VALUE IN VISIONS

ALI WILLIAMS

ALSO BY ALI WILLIAMS

GODSTOUCHED UNIVERSE

The Freed Hunt

Forged in Flames

Value in Visions

Married in Moonlight

Shifting in Secret

Rooted in Ruin

Floating in Fear

Moon Magick

Married in Moonlight

Blue Moon Magic

New Moon Magick

Full Moon Magick

OTHER BOOKS

The Softest Kinksters Collection

Kink the Halls

Value in Visions: A Godstouched Sapphic Romance
Married in Moonlight: A Godstouched Sapphic Short Story
Published by Claficionado Press Ltd
© 2023 Ali Williams

All rights reserved.

This is a work of fiction. Names, characters, places, and incidents either are the products of the author's imagination or are used fictitiously. Any resemblance to actual persons, living or dead, businesses, companies, events, or locales is entirely coincidental.

No part of this book may be reproduced or modified in any form, including photocopying, recording, or by any information storage and retrieval system, without express written permission from the author, except for the use of brief quotations in a review.

Cover design © 2022 Wolfsparrow Covers

For my Nanna and Nonno, reunited at last.

AUTHOR NOTE

Value in Visions includes explicit sex, including praise kink, cunnilingus, and fingering. It also contains references to PTSD, trauma, violence and death (mainly off-page, and the aftermath of some on page, but 2000 years before the setting of this action), sexual assault (off-page and only ever alluded to) and suicide (brief description of a memory, not explicitly violent).

Married in Moonlight has references to an off-page suicide, and grief.

I hope I have treated Aerten, Rina and Andraste's experiences and emotions with the care that they and you deserve.

VALUE IN VISIONS

A GODSTOUCHED SAPPHIC ROMANCE

ALI WILLIAMS

CHAPTER ONE

RINA NEVER THOUGHT the day would come when working in the Tunford Library seemed boring to her, but that day seemed to have actually arrived.

That's not to say that Tunford Library was usually a thriving source of drama; she'd been working there since she'd finished university, and the most exciting thing that had happened in all of that time had been when one of the toddlers had made a bid for freedom during a Read and Rhyme session, and decided to run headlong into every display case that they'd had up. But it was busy. There were days when the library felt like the centre of the village community, and they'd swapped silence and the archetypical librarian 'shhh' for a low-level hum of conversation and work. And she liked that, she really did. What she did mattered. Helping Mrs Alleyne write her sister in Barbados an email; introducing children to the world of books for the first time; showing people how they could use computers to fill out job applications. That mattered. But today it felt boring.

She blamed Kenna.

Rina moved the book trolley round the corner to the crime section and began absent-mindedly shelving returns. It wasn't really her best friend's fault, she knew that, but all of a sudden, their lives had been disrupted by goddesses and dragons and the Wild Hunt and now, in the aftermath of what Arlee had taken to calling 'The Battle of the Forge', everything seemed a little…mundane. The rest of the village, the rest of the *world*, was just carrying on, oblivious to the life-changing knowledge that she was now party to. That gods were real. That their new friends in the village had once been immortal. That she now had visions.

Though there hadn't been so much as a flicker of a vision since everything had died down. That, Rina knew, was the real reason she felt bored right now. She'd had this surge of power that allowed her to see things, visions that mapped out paths forward and flashes of the past. An oracle, Morcant had called her. Kenna's two millennia-old boyfriend seemed pretty certain about that. He and the other members of the Wild Hunt had seemed inclined to fuss when Rina said that she hadn't had any more visions, but she'd put a stop to that, sharpish. Besides, she wasn't fussed about the power aspect of it. The knowledge though…having access to knowledge like that was addictive, and Rina kind of missed it.

No. It was more than that; it was an almost tangible absence in her life and she was not a fan of feeling as if something was missing.

She'd tried to jump start it, but for some reason the magical connection seemed lacking and she'd felt like a bit of a fool, picking up random objects and trying to will a vision into existence. She'd even tried occasionally picking up something that Sten – the silent white-haired Viking – or Deuroc – the smooth-talker who was still attempting to chat up Tegan, the Golden Martlet's landlady – had held, to see if she could sense anything from there, but to no avail. She'd decided *not* to try and read Morcant due to the fact that he and Kenna seemed to be shagging every spare minute they got, and Rina really didn't need have that image of her best friend burned onto the back of her retinas, and similarly their defacto leader Herla looked so harrowed that she just didn't want to see what had put that look into his eyes.

She would have had more luck with Aerten. Rina wasn't entirely certain how she knew that, but knew it she did, even if the point was moot. The red-haired woman had been steadfastly avoiding her.

There'd been that moment before the battle, when Rina had sworn in Italian and had been met with such fury in Aerten's voice and eyes. Fury that had burnt itself out pretty damn quickly, but it had still hurt. Rina had met anger with anger of her own, only to see the life that she'd come to associate with the redhead fade until she was this quiet, withdrawn figure who wouldn't meet her gaze.

Rina paused for a moment, hand in mid-air. If it weren't for the fact that Aerten had specifically guarded Rina with flailing spinning axes during the forge battle, she'd have sworn that the warrior woman hated her. And she still wasn't entirely certain that she didn't. There was something there, but it was something that Aerten didn't want her to see and therefore it seemed unfair to try.

And so, she'd turned to the one thing she was really rather damn good at. Research. She'd researched the fuck out of oracles, but books and even the internet oscillated between being incredibly vague, and implying that it was a state reached only by chaste virgins who were prepared to give up their life in service of their god or goddess. Considering how Kenna's life had been turned so completely upside down by the goddess Belisama, that was one solution that Rina would not be utilising thank you very much.

So she'd settled into this new normal. Or back to the old normal. Days at the library, evenings relaxing at the pub or at home, and every Sunday a big family meal with the whole Baroni clan. It just all felt a little flat, especially when compared to the experience of attempting to stop some power-hungry god from burning up your best friend.

The one thing that had brought a little bit of interest into her life, had been helping the Wild Hunt – or the Freed Hunt, as Deuroc had nicknamed them – to find new jobs. As thanks for their help, the goddess Belisama had magicked pasts into existence for them – and not pasts that consisted of riding around in the hinterland for centuries – and it had been all Rina could do to bring them up to the present day. They'd needed to find jobs, learn how to use technology, and turn the house that Belisama had conjured up into a home, and she'd thrown herself into organising it all for them. If she kept going, kept moving, she wouldn't have time to fret too much about the ache of emptiness that she felt whenever she stopped for too long.

She felt vaguely protective of them all, settling into their new lives as mortals once more, and may or may not have turned up on their doorstep with the odd lasagne or sausage casserole for them to eat. None of them seemed particularly proficient at cooking – not exactly a key skill when you hadn't eaten for centuries – but the Italian in Rina couldn't allow them to go hungry. She suspected that when they ran out of whatever large meal she brought over at the beginning of the week, they primarily lived on takeout, but Tunford was small, and aside from her family's restaurant, the pub and the Chinese takeaway, options were limited.

Still, she wanted to know, *needed* to know, that they'd all be okay. The disruption had shuddered through all of their lives, and she longed to be able to just peer into the future and tell that it would all be okay.

"Well, I could help you with that."

The voice behind her was unfamiliar, and Rina blinked rapidly and pushed her glasses firmly up her nose before turning round to face its speaker.

The woman before her had an animal pelt flung around her shoulders, with a golden torc adorning her neck, blonde hair braided back, and the most vivid blue make up smeared across her face. And the look on that face wasn't what Rina would have described as kind. She looked haughty, as if the whole library, and everyone in it, were beneath her. Everyone including Rina, although she appeared to consider Rina less on a par with dirt.

"For a Godstouched, you seem more than a little awe-struck by the presence of a goddess in your midst."

Fuck, thought Rina. Out loud she said nothing, but moved so that the two of them were tucked behind a display, in the hope that they'd be able to avoid scrutiny and someone kicking up a fuss about the woman wearing what she suspected was actually real fur in the library.

"Well?"

She sighed and met the woman's eyes head on. They were shimmering slightly, as if behind the brown Rina could see images and battlefields and blood. Lots and lots of blood. She withheld a shudder as best she could; showing fear didn't seem like the best of ideas. "Which goddess?"

The goddess stepped up until her face was almost touching Rina's, and not in a fun-sexy-I'm-going-to-kiss-you kind of way. This was giving off distinct mind-what-you-say-or-I'll-headbutt-you vibes. *"Andraste the Indestructible."*

"The Indestructible? Very cool." She was clearly a warrior goddess of some kind, though the name conjured up images of barbarian heroes rather than deities. The goddess' head moved a fraction and for a second Rina wondered whether she'd gone too far and was going to have to try and explain away a broken nose to her mother, but then she stepped back and was looking at Rina thoughtfully.

"You're not scared of me. This is good. It will make your working for me easier."

Rina cleared her throat pointedly. "Thank you, but no thank you."

"What?" Andraste strode forward again, and this time Rina side-stepped her quite neatly and took a book off a shelf with a hand that only betrayed her emotions with the slightest of tremors. She examined the spine deliberately, and then moved it to its correct position further along the shelf. Small steps. Simple actions that connected her to the here and now and meant that she didn't throw some poor unsuspecting tome at the goddess' head and run away screaming.

"The offer is kind, but I have a job already."

The look that the goddess shot her wasn't even straight on, but it still managed to send those terrifying tremors from her hand scurrying across Rina's body. Her knees shook and she locked them into place so she couldn't fall over. Well that was just rude. Quietly but firmly she said, "This is my place of work."

Andraste threw a dismissive glance around them. *"What are words in the face of real action?"*

Now that really was uncalled for. Real action indeed. What would someone who was indestructible know about 'real action' anyway? Surely it was all much of a muchness if you couldn't be killed? "Words," she bit out, her voice short, "have been the basis of my career."

"Oracles work in visions, not in words."

And there it was, the real reason why this goddess had decided to grace Tunford's tiny library with her presence.

"No."

"*No?*"

"No. I don't know you, and I don't know what you'd want to use my visions for. So, no." Not everyone realised that Rina had a stubborn streak until they came up against it, and then they realised that no pleading or arguing would budge her on the matter in hand. Especially if she were being *told* to do something. The only person who could tell her what to do was Lenna, Head Librarian, and the Black woman was perceptive enough to recognise when Rina wasn't going to back down over something and usually switched course.

Andraste reached out and grabbed Rina's arm, her touch icy but firm, and no matter how Rina tugged, she could not pull away. *"You* will *have visions for me, oracle. I'd advise you take the easy route."*

But there was no way that she was going to let someone come into her library, the place she felt most comfortable, and start ordering her around. It simply wasn't going to happen. Or at least, it wasn't going to continue happening.

"I'm afraid," she said, in that stern librarian tone that she only brought out for those occasions when she was really pissed off, "that I'm going to have to ask you to leave the premises."

The icy grip around her wrist tightened.

"And," she continued, letting a little of her annoyance seep into her voice, "you should let go of me." She felt her temper flare and almost instantly, the hand around her wrist was gone.

The goddess glared at her. *"You will regret this; I promise. And I shall not be so lenient again."*

Rina merely turned her back on the woman and walked away saying "I'm sure you can see yourself out, just as you saw yourself in." She shook off the uncomfortable feeling that she'd set something in motion that she wouldn't be able to reverse. Rina rubbed at her arm distractedly, where that cold touch had seeped through her skin. Perhaps it would be too much to hope that the goddess would now leave her alone, but at least she hadn't agreed to any vision-making service.

CHAPTER TWO

ADJUSTING TO HAVING A JOB WAS...INTERESTING.

Before Herla and his Hunt had picked her and her sister up off the battlefield, Aerten had been a leader. Her father the leader of the Iceni, her mother Boudicca. And no matter what had happened in that Roman betrayal, she had still remained a figure of respect. A woman to be followed.

Only now she spent her evenings picking up men off the floor who deemed it appropriate to leer at her, and say such things that would make a whore blush. Admittedly, she was almost always the one who put them there in the first place. She found that a stiff arm worked quite well when you had someone running right at you, and she did find the slinging-them-out-the-door after the picking-them-up-off-the-floor bit quite satisfying.

It was not like that in the Golden Martlet, of course. Tegan was formidable as a landlady, and Aerten's work mainly comprised of gently steering drunken farmers out the door at the end of the night, but the – shifts, she believed they were called – at the establishment in the very large, very loud, town had been eye-opening.

As had the women. Aerten had always had an eye for ladies, appreciative of their soft curves and softer smiles, and these women were completely open in their friendliness. Openly affectionate with each other, and often teasing her til she flushed in a way that the cruder remarks from other patrons could never elicit. Part of her wanted to experience it for herself one night, to go dancing with a lass, but she couldn't shake the feeling that it wasn't quite safe. There were always predators out, and it wasn't just women who were their target.

It had been Arlee who'd found her this job, and they had sat her down beforehand and explained that she would have to keep an eye out for those who ventured out merely to cause trouble, and particularly cause trouble for those in what they called the queer community. Aerten found that she didn't much care who she was looking after, as long as she lived up to the job title of security guard. She took that very seriously, both the guarding part of her job and the providing of security.

She'd bristled at the commands she'd been given at first, by men with less experience on the battlefield than she, but soon realised that this modern world was far more complex than she'd given it credit, and sticking to her role and 'bouncing' as Arlee called it, was the best use of her time.

Still, it did rankle. She'd helped her mother lead hordes of men into battle, her throat hoarse from war cries, her heart pounding in time with the thudding hoof beats of the horses pulling her chariot, and she was having to adapt.

The rest of the Wild Hunt, that motley troop of men whom she'd grown quietly fond of, had never had any reason to order her around. Herla wasn't her king the way he was for Morcant and Deuroc, and had never tried to impose his rule upon her, and Sten had fought alongside enough shieldmaidens in his time to recognise a fellow warrior. And that was just as well really. She didn't think she'd have responded well to orders. Brianne might have been different but-

Aerten cut off her thoughts.

No. She had things in the here and now to focus on. A dead sister, however beloved, would only distract her from the task at hand. Door duty on a Saturday night in central Brighton. Apparently, some hen dos had booked tables for the night, and even the most hardened of bouncers on her team had blanched at the thought of it and had seemed eager to let her test herself. She'd felt more than a little disappointment when she realised that she would merely have to handle a gaggle of women out for the night, and wasn't entirely certain what they'd been so worried about.

Holding out a hand, she took the identification from the first pink-adorned woman and examined it. Acceptable. She handed it back, and stood aside to let them pass which they did with an entirely unnecessary bout of giggles. She raised an eyebrow before turning back. Next.

BY THE TIME Aerten was done for the night, she had re-evaluated her assessment of hen dos. Thoroughly.

There'd been the women decked in fake penises who'd tried to grope all the men on the premises, consenting or not, someone who'd downed an entire tray of shots and then vomited all over the outside seating, and – which had been the final straw – one woman who'd decided that slapping Aerten's arse had been an appropriate course of action. Even the leering men she usually detested had stopped short of that. She'd never been so horrified at such behaviour.

"Cis straight white girls," Robin said as way of explanation, when she asked him what the hell was going on.

"They get drunk, come into town for a night, and throw their privilege all over the place."

"It's appalling."

He smiled wryly, "Wait until Pride."

She vowed to avoid Pride, whatever it was, like the damn plague.

Stepping away from the club and breathing in that salty sea air had been a tonic after a night of averting near disasters. Aerten had wandered down to the seafront to lean against the guardrails and look out to where the waves were cresting the shore. The shuckle of pebbles being dragged back and forth calmed her and she sighed. It was the favourite part of her night really. Where she got to walk away from the chaos and just be for those ten minutes, before sitting astride her bike and riding home.

Arlee had taught Aerten how to ride a motorbike, claiming that an independent means of transport was vital when travelling home late after work, and she'd discovered that she loved it. It had been a surprise because she'd always been a horse person, but this was like riding a horse. just faster and with large vibrating metal between her legs, which may or may not have provoked sensations that brought colour to her cheeks in not an unsatisfying manner. Aerten suspected that part of its appeal was the ability to up and leave whenever she wanted. Fed up of Herla grumping about at home? Go for a ride. Need some extra food from the shop? Head on out. Avoid the dark-haired Italian woman who haunted her dreams? Go flying across country lanes with the wind buffeting her and the bike.

She straddled the bike now, adjusting her helmet and her driving gloves as that knot in her stomach tightened in anticipation.

This was the real reason she loved riding the bike – because it felt like riding a chariot. All of that power beneath your hands, coiled and ready to spring forward into action. It left her on such a high when she got home, that she had to release that tension before she could get any sleep. She was rather fond of her new night routine.

And then she was off. First winding her way through narrow streets which opened up, eventually giving way to countryside roads nestled in fields and hedgerow. So remote that the only light came from her headlight and the stars above. But the darkness was rich in its velvety shadow, and she revelled in it. She'd take this over the washed-out grayscale that the Hunt had been trapped in for millennia. That world, the world behind the Veil, had always felt suffocating for her – no matter how grateful she'd been for the reprieve from death. It had been bearable at first, when she'd had her sister beside her. The two of them had finally been able to ride away from their shadows, leaving the horror of their nightmares behind, for the world behind the Veil had no dreams. But then that had become a nightmare in itself.

Aerten shook her head and looked out across the rolling hills of the South Downs. None of them quite knew what it was that had made the Veil here so gossamer thin, allowing them to slip back through, two millennia later, but she knew she was glad for it. The home they were making for themselves, in the small village of Tunford, was one with light and laughter. A small village for people with open hearts. No one seemed to question where they'd come from, but were just grateful that they were there.

She put that down in no small part to Belisama. The goddess had come through on her promise to make it appear as if they'd always been a part of this world, and Aerten was determined to make the most of it. Yes, she might only really want to head into the city for work, and would rather have spent all of her time in the relative quiet of Tunford, but there were more ways to live than just cramming yourself in amongst as many people as possible.

Actually, her first aim was to work out how this machine worked. Because she wanted to be able to fix it if it broke, and she really rather liked the idea of being able to spend her days working with her hands on it. That would be most satisfying.

Pulling up to the house where the Hunt now lived, she parked in the driveway and turned her bike off, feeling the thrum of its engine slowly die before heading up smartly to the front door. It was late, but all of the Hunt were still adjusting to nights without sleep, so she was unsurprised to hear voices coming from their communal living room.

"Ah, the wanderer returns! How was your night in the big city?" Deuroc was laughing at her, she knew.

"Probably less smelly than your day on the farm. Did the baby goat attack you again?"

Deuroc's smiling face froze. "Don't Aerten, please. That little terror is the bane of my existence. I don't understand why he hates me so much."

She laughed as she took off her leathers. He really was having a hard time of it. He was lounging on one of the sofas and she threw herself onto the one opposite, sinking down into the cushions with an audible sigh of relief. "Gods this is comfortable."

There wasn't much of an answer, Deuroc apparently still caught up in painful memories of baby goats. Looking around, she saw Herla in a corner, whittling a piece of wood with sharp, angry movements, his hair surrounding his face like a veil. Still in a bad mood then. Herla had had the strangest attitude since their freedom, toasting to this new world one moment, and sullen and silent the next. At least Sten's silence was calming. She glanced over to where he sat by the fire, keeping an eye on its glowing embers. They'd all been relieved to find that Belisama had brought a house with a proper fireplace into existence; there was something comforting and very grounding about building a fire, and expending energy in keeping it alight, and it was something so familiar that even though their new friends had been a little baffled at their enthusiasm, they'd been excited for them.

Thinking of the trio who'd welcomed them and stood by their side against Belenus, she smiled. Each of them had helped in their own way. Kenna had done more than enough already, what with forging her blood with theirs in order to free them all, plus there was the added benefit of her being the love of Morcant's life. Arlee gave lessons, both of the driving and the reading kind, though the basic groundwork seemed to have been laid by Belisama, which really, they had Rina to thank for. Rina. Rina was the one who worried about them the most, the one who turned up to help in whatever way she could so often that it was getting difficult to avoid her. And she was also the one who brought food with her.

She shot a look at Deuroc. "I don't suppose that anyone's done dinner?"

"Just leftovers from yesterday in the fridge."

"Good." Jumping up, she headed to the kitchen to where homemade lasagne was waiting for her. Aerten had been secretly hoping that they hadn't polished all of it off, because they'd had it for the first time the night before and Gods it was amazing. Simple ingredients, but married together in a harmony that her mouth wanted her to sing. She'd never really been a food person – there's only so many ways to stew meat – but now? She could taste Rina in the cooking, the care and the friendship that she unknowingly stirred into each dish, and if she couldn't face her in person, at least she could do this, take comfort in the food that Rina showed her affection through.

She heaped a large portion into a bowl and popped it in the microwave, counting down the seconds until she'd get that delicious taste all to herself. But before the machine could ping, there was a hammering on the front door. Not just a knock. Hammering.

Cursing late visitors under her breath, Aerten headed over and opened the door to see a wild-eyed Rina on her doorstep. Her usually tidy hair was a mess, as if she'd dragged her hands through it over and over, and those dark eyes looked up at her with such desperate pleading that made Aerten want to drop everything and destroy the person who'd put that look there. Her heart clenched as a single tear made its way down Rina's cheek.

"Aerten." Rina's voice cracked and she blinked furiously, sending more tears spilling down her cheeks. "It's the goddess. She's kidnapped my brother."

CHAPTER THREE

SHE DIDN'T REALISE until Aerten had opened the door, how much she'd wanted her to be there. The other members of the Hunt were great, sure, but Aerten was the one who'd protected her before, standing guard outside the office door during the fight earlier that summer, and Rina was self-aware enough to acknowledge that she seemed to associate the other woman with safety as a result.

And she needed safety right now.

She'd been locking up the library for the night when her mother had called her in a complete state, worrying about the fact that Alessandro hadn't come home from school yet. Rina hadn't been too worried herself; her brother was fourteen years old and had probably gone to hang out with one of his friends after school. Sandro didn't hate the family business, but what teenager wanted to spend their evenings helping out in a busy restaurant? But her mother was worried and so it was a case of Baronis assemble! Her sister, Bianca, had actually delegated in the kitchen for once, and had stepped out from behind the pass to look for him.

It hadn't been until they'd called round the parents of his

school friends – something that Rina suspected that Sandro would not thank them for later – and checked in all his usual hangouts, that she suddenly had an unshakeable feeling. One of *those* unshakeable feelings.

She'd sat in her car and forced herself to lean into it. To really push that feeling as far as it would go and she'd had this image of Sandro's tear-streaked face, angry in defiance, looking up as falling soil fell down. And that was when she knew.

This was that fucking goddess.

"The goddess? What goddess?" Aerten's face was tense, and she gripped Rina's shoulders.

The sudden contact had her jerking to look up into the other woman's eyes. She saw her reflection there, despairing, and almost shuddered at the open vulnerability on her own face. She was not in control here, not calm and collected, and damn if that wasn't completely obvious. "Andraste."

For a moment, Rina saw burning fury in Aerten's eyes, the same furious anger that she'd seen in the battle at the forge, but instead of shrinking away, she found herself moving forward. Emboldened by that energy. "You know her."

"I know her." Aerten's voice was flat and cold, but her eyes warmed in something akin to sympathy. "Come in. I'll help you find your brother."

At the beginning of the day, if anyone had asked Rina if she'd have turned to Aerten for comfort, she'd have laughed in their face. Aerten was not unkind, but she was distant and had definitely made it clear that she wanted nothing to do with Rina. Only here she was, a tall figure striding down the hallway to the kitchen, waving away the men who stood questioning in the doorway to the living room, and gathering Rina up and putting a bowl of her own lasagne down in front of her.

"Eat. It's good for shock."

She watched as the woman warmed another bowl. Decisive movements. And it was comforting watching her, realising that she'd already thought about everything that she was going to do, and clearly had plans on what to do next.

When Aerten noticed Rina watching her, she raised an eyebrow and nodded towards the bowl.

With a quiet smile, Rina began to eat.

She was grateful for the bowl in front of her. Growing up in a large loud Italian family meant that food was at the heart of everything. Eating together, with everyone talking over everyone else; cooking together, learning how to shape the perfect gnocchi or just when to add grappa to the sugo; and feeding each other. She knew her family loved her, and she knew it because when she'd had her heart broken, and when her hamster had died, and when she'd had exams, they'd each turn up, laden down with food to go in the freezer or a bowl of stellina en brodo or a mountain of profiteroles.

So she couldn't help but feel a little bit loved by Aerten too.

Not in *that* way, obviously, but Rina associated food and being fed with care, and she could sense Aerten's need to care for her.

They ate in relative silence, side by side, and Aerten didn't speak until they'd both cleared not just one, but two bowls each of lasagne. "So. Tell me about Andraste."

AERTEN LISTENED to everything Rina had to say. Quietly.

That wasn't easy, by the way, being quiet and listening to how that bitch of a goddess had swept back into this world and ruined another family's existence. It was fucking difficult.

Rina's voice was trembly, but there was an edge of defiance as she told her story that made Aerten flush with something akin to pride. She would, however, have been proud of anyone who'd stood their ground when faced with an ancient goddess. The fact that that anyone had come in a package that was small but perfectly formed – dark hair, darker eyes, and a lithe frame that-

Aerten stopped that thought right there. No. She could not afford to have such thoughts.

"How do you know her?" Those dark eyes were fixed on her and Aerten had a hard time looking away.

"She interfered with my family too." Interfered was such an understatement that the word tasted bitter on Aerten's tongue, but she didn't want to worry Rina more and so she stopped, momentarily caught in a web of memories where everything brought her back to that one battlefield, over and over again.

There was a short pause and then Rina pulled herself up straight in her chair and raised an eyebrow, "Really. That's all you're going to tell me?"

"It happened centuries ago; are you really sure that storytelling at such a time is the correct course of action?" She knew that she was being a little obtuse, but if she could get away with not having to go into details...

This time, the dark eyes flashed and Rina pushed herself up to standing. "Would you seriously be asking that same question if it were a member of your family who was missing? Truthfully?"

Aerten sighed and reached out to grasp Rina's hand, entangling their fingers together and tugged gently until she sat down again. "This isn't easy for me," she tried, as way of explanation, though the truth was that in some ways the story had been burning at the back of her throat for centuries, longing to springboard off her tongue out into the world. "It's not nice and it's not pretty and it brings up memories that I'd really rather forget."

She felt the thud of her heart then, echoing through her body the way it had when she'd been in her chariot, riding forward, leading with her mother, and she involuntarily tightened her grip on the hand she didn't realise that she was still holding.

Head bent, she heard Rina shuffle her chair forward, and then long untidy brown curls ghosted where their hands met.

"Aerten," said Rina, her voice gentle, as if she were afraid that speaking at volume would shatter this uneasy trust between them, "You don't have to tell me everything. Maybe just the bits that might be relevant? If you're not ready-"

"If I'm not ready now, when will I be?" The words burst from Aerten and, voice unstoppered for the first time, a torrent of sentences followed it. "I have to be ready. I should be ready. It's been too long, too many years since all of this— And she's back now. She's back *now* and she's hurting you and yours and I just will not let that happen. I cannot."

A quick flicker of a glance at Rina showed the brunette sat there, blinking a little in the wake of such an avalanche of words. Aerten froze. Forced herself to slowly unfurl her body and sit up a little straighter. Compose herself. But when she went to let go of Rina's hand, the other woman didn't let go. She held on.

"We should really talk to you guys about seeing a therapist," said Rina thoughtfully.

"A therapist?"

"Someone who you talk about your problems and stresses to. I get the impression that you're all holding a lot back, and it's not always healthy to just purge it all at once."

Aerten wasn't quite sure what to make of that. Everyone had problems and stresses, so what good would talking about it do? Although she knew that wasn't quite true. Talking about things should help. Would have helped, if she hadn't been so used to centuries of riding with stubborn warriors who refused to emote or engage with their feelings.

"Okay." It was clear that Rina had made a decision, and Aerten found herself smiling a little, despite everything. "You don't need to tell me everything, because it's clear that that would be pretty traumatic for you and I'm not a professional; we could end up doing more damage than good. How about you stick to just the bits about Andraste that you remember. And if anything becomes too much, you just tell me and we shift gears."

Aerten stared at her. "But your family-"

"Are hardly likely to be helped by your reliving your trauma, but I would appreciate you sharing the little details with me that you can recall."

The requested floored Aerten. The little details were the things that she'd forgotten in the wake of feeling so utterly betrayed by the one being they thought they could all trust. The little details meant trying to remember the good things, the things that happened before it all went wrong.

"She is a warrior goddess," she started, the words now slow to her tongue, "so not as nice as Belisama."

"Belisama is nice?" interjected Rina. "What about the whole nearly killing Kenna thing?"

Aerten laughed, the sound sharp and bitter. "Yes, but she wasn't intending to do that. Andraste...Andraste is who you call when you want revenge. She's the one to whom you loose a hare before battle. She's the one to whom you sacrifice all of your captives. She's the one whose woodland grove is strung up in blood."

When she took a breath, she realised that Rina was

staring at her, wide-eyed, and looking more than a little panicky. "And she has my brother?!"

Shit. She'd forgotten that vital piece of information for a moment. "Yes, but she took your brother for a reason. She wants you to come to her, and he's just a way of getting to that goal. She won't hurt him before then; it won't occur to her to do so. Death outside of battle or the spoils of war isn't really her style."

Rina looked a little less frantic at that, thank goodness, but she'd also let go of Aerten's hand, and Aerten was feeling its absence acutely.

"So how do you know Andraste? Did you worship her?"

Ah.

She thought for a moment, trying to work out how best to explain the next bit. "What do you know of Boudicca?"

"The Queen of the Iceni? Faced down the Romans?"

"So you know some."

"Of course, she's one of the first female historical figures we're taught about as children at school."

Aerten's breath caught in her throat and she forced it out, slowly. When she looked up, she noticed that Rina was looking at her in alarm, and when she raised a hand to her cheeks, it came away damp. "She'd have liked that."

"You knew her?" Rina's eyes were wide, "I mean, I know you've all been around for millennia, but the fact that you actually *knew* Boudicca is, well, wow."

It really hit her then, that her history was remembered even now. That to be associated with Boudicca was something of wonder, something to be celebrated. How long had it been since she'd thought of her past with anything but anger and heartbreak?

"She was my mother."

The words sat between them, until Aerten spoke again, rushing this time. "She was the one who laid offerings before

Andraste, asked her for her aid in avenging the violence and the horror that our people endured. That we endured. And the goddess granted us her blessing, watched as we did so much in her name, as we-" She broke off this time, unable to speak of what they had done for the goddess, what they had done on and off the battlefield, and this time it was Rina's hand that reached for hers.

It gave her strength, the warmth of her fingers against Aerten's palm calming her, allowing her took take breaths and centre herself again. "She abandoned us in that last battle and they slaughtered us. Only myself and my sister survived, barely alive, to be picked out from the carnage by the Wild Hunt." She turned then, to look at Rina. "I thought that I had to survive, had to live, for my mother and my clan and my people, so that they would live on through me. But you say that they are already remembered? That our histories are our own?"

"Yes."

"Thank you."

CHAPTER FOUR

WELL, that had been a whole revelation.

Rina wasn't sure whether she was more furious on behalf of herself and her family, or Aerten and hers. What was clear though, was that Andraste needed to be stopped. Rina decided that she was going to find her brother, give the goddess a talking to, and preferably shove her back from whence she came.

But first, she thought, looking down at where her hand lay in Aerten's, she should work out how best to help Aerten. Those resurfacing memories had clearly taken a toll on her. Rina squeezed her hand, "Are you okay?"

No sooner had she asked the question, than a bright smile slammed down across Aerten's features. "Of course. Does that help?"

She looked at the redhead, frowning, "You know that it's okay *not* to be okay, right? You don't need to pretend around me."

The brightness dimmed a little, and Aerten sat a less straight in her chair. "I- I can't not be okay right now."

That made sense. Rina'd had her own fair share of if-I-stop-I'll-break moments, so she recognised a coping mechanism when she saw it. And this was definitely a coping mechanism, even if it was creaky as fuck, and the cogs in the mechanism were rusty and need re-oiling, so she nodded and said brightly, "Okay, so I need a plan of action, if we're going to find my brother without getting entangled in Andraste's web. Do you want to crash now and then plan tomorrow, or are you up for some night-time exploits?"

She could see that it took a moment for it to sink in for Aerten that she wasn't going to push it, and when it did an actual smile spread across her face that made Rina want to always make her smile, just like that.

Rina wasn't usually a very cuddly person. She was practical and she was sensible and she came up with organised plans based on research, but right now she wanted to just clamber into Aerten's lap and nuzzle at her neck until the redhead smiled and stroked her hair. She wanted to be petted and loved and cared for and she was beginning to realise that she wanted Aerten to be the one doing the petting and loving and caring.

"You want to plan now?"

She flushed, the words interrupting her thoughts and nodded.

"Well fuck sleep then, let's get started."

AERTEN WASN'T ENTIRELY certain how their planning had led them here, to a locked and darkened building in the middle of the night.

"Don't move," Rina had hissed, before she'd walked carefully across the open hallway to where a panel was bleeping. Some urgent jabbing resulted in the bleeping ceasing, and she turned the lights back on before turning round to Aerten, almost beaming in pride.

"I don't think you've ever been to my library before, have you?"

"Your library?" Aerten couldn't help grinning when faced with Rina's infectious enthusiasm.

"Yes, my library." She nodded and then gestured Aerten through ahead of her. "Welcome to my world."

Aerten had never seen anything quite like it.

It was a huge room, slanted roof leading up to where stars twinkled through a large skylight, with what she assumed were other rooms, leading off it, but its construction was nothing compared to what it contained.

Books.

Hundreds and hundreds of books. Thousands even.

Aerten had seen books before – you don't traverse the countryside for centuries without picking up on changes in advances – and they'd all been trying to use them a little more since they'd been freed, but it had felt like a luxury to her. To have something that held so much potential, so much knowledge, in the palm of her hand felt truly decadent. But they'd soon realised that in this world where you could to talk to people through a box in your hand, books weren't all that special. They were an old technology that many didn't love as much as she and the rest of the Freed Hunt did.

But this room.

"How many?"

"Over ten thousand."

She marvelled at the thought. "And you work here? This is where you spend your days?"

Rina laughed, "It's not usually as quiet as this; it kind of works as a hub of the community, so we do more than just books." She paused, "but the books are what I love the most.

Come," and she took Aerten's hand and pulled her this way and that through the shelving.

It was, Aerten thought, the thing that she was coming to like the most about Rina; the fact that she held her hand. All of them in the Hunt had spent so many centuries starved of physical affection, that it meant something now. The mere touch of Rina's hand in hers was doing things to Aerten's head that not one pretty lass dressed for a night out had done in all her weeks working security. Her hair was all over the place and she was drowning in that oversized hooded jumper that she wore, but every time their fingers touched Aerten just wanted to pull Rina close and wrap her in her arms.

Rina was running her finger across the spines of the books until there was a little crow of victory as she pulled a volume off the shelf. "This is what I used last time."

"Last time?"

"The first time I had a vision," she explained. "I was trying to find out information about dragons and the map just unfurled before me and showed me the way, so this could be just like that."

Aerten wasn't so certain that it was going to be as simple as all that, but she wasn't going to dampen Rina's hopes, so she said nothing and just watched.

Rina laid the book out flat on the table next to the shelf, and stared at it, almost as if she were daring it to open.

Nothing.

She gave a small noise of frustration, and then flipped it open herself, flicking through pages until she came to the back, "The index," she explained to Aerten, "of all the places in Sussex," and then began running her index finger down column after column of text, turning pages with increasing velocity until Aerten reached out and moved the book away before a page ripped.

"What?"

The face that was upturned now was furiously focused and Aerten felt like she may have taken her life in her hands by interrupting. She tried to speak, but had to clear her throat a few times before the words would venture out in front of this Rina. "Last time you knew what you were looking for, yes? Maybe if you had something of your brother's to hold?"

Rina blinked, the focus abating just for a moment, and then she reached into the pocket of her hoodie and pulled out a scarf. It was a small scarf – the hoodie wasn't *that* oversized –delicate and covered in butterflies and she smiled down at it before placing it on the table.

"A Christmas present," she said as way of explanation, "Sandro bought it for me last year."

Maybe that would help? Aerten wasn't sure, but anything was better than watching Rina tear through a book in mounting desperation.

This time Rina took a breath and closed her eyes before picking up the scarf and wrapping it round her neck, and then opened the book flat in her palms. It was almost as if a hush fell over the library, as if something or someone was waiting, and Aerten's palms itched for axes to weight them, and lend her some strength to protect the woman in front of her.

The book slammed shut with a snap and then Rina, eyes open but unseeing, started walking off down the stacks, murmuring to herself so quietly that Aerten couldn't make out what she was saying.

This was creepy, she realised. She'd never seen an oracle in action before, and she was struck with fear for Rina herself, that whatever she was channelling would be too powerful and too dangerous for her mortal body to cope with. Hurrying around the corner, she saw Rina pulling a different book off the shelf and then everything seemed to let out a sigh and Rina was there, herself again.

Without meaning to, Aerten strode over, her hands either side of Rina's shoulders and said "Are you okay? Rina, *are you okay?*"

It wasn't until she saw Rina's stunned expression, that she realised that she'd been shouting. Her hands dropped to her sides, and she moved away quickly, not wanting to see the upset in the brunette's eyes, but there was that hand again, slipping into hers, and when she looked down at Rina, Rina was smiling up at her. "I'm okay Aerten, I promise. It's kind of like seeing layers over everything around me, but it doesn't hurt."

Her gruff response was one of relief, and Rina squeezed her hand in comfort. "I'm all good, and look – I have an actual clue!"

THE BOOK that Rina had found had actually been pretty clear. She'd floated through some kind of haze until her hand had found the right book on the shelf and as soon as she saw the title, the haze had lifted, and she'd known exactly where they needed to go. Kind of.

Barrows of Sussex.

"Barrows?" asked Aerten.

"Yes, they're these Neolithic monuments or burial mounds, from before even your time though."

"Ah, the beorg…"

She looked up at Aerten then, and said, "I'd like to try and see if there's any specific barrow that they'd like us to look at, there are tons spread out all over the South Downs, but it means focusing again."

The redhead brusquely moved a strand of hair from where it had fallen across Rina's eyes and nodded. "Of course. Thank you for, you know-"

"Giving you a heads up?" Rina shook her head, "Not a problem at all. Right, step back a bit." With one hand she grasped the scarf, and with the other she balanced the book on its spine. "Let's see if we can get us closer to Sandro."

And then it was coming over her again, that feeling of knowledge just beyond her fingertips, filling up her all the way up to her pores until she wasn't sure whether or not she was sweating it out of her skin. The book fell open and she let go of the scarf to grab it in both hands before it closed, looking down to see where the pages had fallen.

Lewes.

It was a start. A good start, but there were – she squinted down at the page – over 70 different barrows in the district of Lewes. Fuck.

She felt her hand clench around the spine of the book and all of the stress and worry for Sandro, all of the anxiety that she'd somehow managed to stave off for the last hour, suddenly started leaking out of her eyes. Tears. Godsdamned tears.

A firm hand took the book out of hers, and pulled her close. She found herself turning her body into Aerten's, her face just above the swell of Aerten's chest, her head fitting just beneath the curve of the other woman's throat. Two warm arms slipped around her, and just held her as she finally let go and just cried.

CHAPTER FIVE

RINA REALLY DIDN'T LIKE CRYING in front of other people. It made her feel awkward and a little embarrassed, and so she found herself pushing away from Aerten after a few minutes, angrily brushing traitorous tears from her eyes.

"I'm not a crier," she said. "I'm a face-the-problem-and-find–a-solution kind of person. Not a break-down-and-cry-over-it kind of person." Okay, so there was a slight irony in the fact that she'd turned up in tears on Aerten's doorstep already that evening, so perhaps she was a crier in extreme circumstances, but even then... She shrugged her shoulders awkwardly. "I'm not a crier."

Aerten nodded. "I believe you."

Rina looked up at the redhead cautiously. "That's very nice of you when there are tear stains on your shirt. I don't think I've ever been more grateful to have not bothered with make up; that could have been a disaster!" Her hand, as awkward as her words, went to brush the tears off Aerten's top, as if that were even possible, and was caught up in the other woman's hand.

"Please. Rina. It's okay."

Their eyes met then and for a moment it felt as if the world had frozen around them. That soft concern in muted grey – Rina opened her mouth to say something, but stopped. Words frozen along with the world. It seemed too nebulous, this moment, to trust to the fickle nature of language that could be misunderstood or misconstrued. And there was nothing about this moment that Rina wanted to be misconstrued.

In this moment, dwarfed in her hoodie, tear stains on her cheeks, hair in the messiest bun that she'd ever constructed, she wanted to be completely understood, just as she was.

This was her.

Something must have shown on her face, because Aerten gave a muttered curse and dropped Rina's hand, only to cup her face in both hands a fraction of a second later. "Serch." Those grey eyes were searching Rina's, plumbing their depths, and they clearly found what they were looking for as Aerten leaned forward and brushed her lips once, twice, against Rina's cheeks, kissing away the tears.

And when Rina angled her face upwards to smile quiet thanks, Aerten's lips were *right there*. Pink and plump and she knew how they felt against her skin, but all Rina could think about was touching her mouth to Aerten's.

So she did.

It wasn't an all-consuming passion kind of a kiss. It was quiet and a little timid, and there was a question in there that Rina needed answered. And answered it was because Aerten kissed her back. This woman with all her fire and passion and history kissed Rina as if she were the most delicate thing she'd ever held. Rina didn't know if she'd ever felt so cherished before.

She found herself holding onto the lapels of Aerten's shirt, fists bunched in material as they kissed, slow and steady and. Ugh. It was a lot. This was a lot.

Aerten must have sensed something shift, because mouths went from clinging to distant, foreheads kissing instead. "Is all well, serch?"

Huffing out a smile, Rina nodded. "That was nice." Eyes still closed, she could hear the smile in Aerten's reply.

"It was indeed."

"But…" she paused, unsure how to go on.

"Timing?"

"Yes." The timing genuinely couldn't have been any worse. They stood there, close in the silence before she drew back suddenly, and met Aerten's gaze, a little panicked. "It's not that I don't want to-"

"I know."

"And it was awesome-"

"It was indeed 'awesome'," the corner of Aerten's mouth tweaked upwards as she tried out the word. "But your brother and the goddess…" Aerten took both of Rina's hands in her own and Rina allowed the tension in her shoulders to dissipate a little. "We shall deal with that first, and us after. And if you would like to be kissed at any point in the meanwhile, my mouth is yours."

SHE'D WAITED for centuries to be kissed, and it had been the sweetest, loveliest thing. Just like the slight brunette before her. So Aerten really didn't mind if romancing had to take a slight backseat whilst they went questing. She could wait for such a kiss again. She would wait another thousand years for another kiss from this lass.

Rina looked vaguely bemused. "So let me get this straight: we're going to face down Andraste, rescue my brother, and all the while I get to have kisses on demand?"

"Ummm…yes?" It hadn't sounded quite so ridiculous when Aerten had said it herself. She'd actually thought it was a little romantic.

"Okay."

"Okay?"

"Okay."

Well, thought Aerten. That was that then. Kisses on demand and sending Andraste spinning back out of their lives. She didn't want to think much about the order of that; years she'd spent furious with the goddess who'd betrayed her people, her mother, her, and one kiss from an Italian speaking brunette and she was prioritising kisses?

But such kisses…

Aerten shook her head, trying to refocus, and in doing so picked up the discarded book and offered it to Rina. "Do you want to try again?"

Rina eyed the book thoughtfully and then suddenly took off past bookshelves, saying over her shoulder, "I'm thinking we should go back to the maps." That made sense; they had a large location already, perhaps Rina would be able to glean something that would help them narrow their focus.

As Rina unfurled the map, laying it down on a table and smoothing out the creases, Aerten went to take a step back.

"Wait."

She stopped, and raised an eyebrow.

"I think," Rina's voice sounded uncertain, "that perhaps maybe I could try whilst holding your hand?"

Aerten's other eyebrow rose in conjunction with her other. Not that she had an issue with holding Rina's hand whilst magic was afoot, but it had been some time since she'd been witness to such things as a regular occurrence and she wasn't sure that she'd ever been a conduit.

"We don't have to if you'd feel uncomfortable," Rina

hastened to add, tripping over her words in the most adorable attempt to reassure Aerten. "It was just an idea-"

"Of course we can try that." She reached out for Rina's hand and warmth flow through her when the other woman's fingers interlaced with hers. "Anything you need." Aerten was fast coming round to the fact that she was likely to agree anything that Rina asked of her. Help save her brother? *Of course.* Face down a warrior goddess? *Why not.* Be a conduit for magical forces? *Whatever you say.*

It wasn't as alarming an experience as Aerten thought it would be, with barely a tingle in her fingers when Rina focused on the map before her, but this time rivulets of blue trickled across the paper. They weren't following river paths, so neither of them knew entirely what it meant until Aerten reached out and touched it.

Woad.

Andraste.

Her other hand, still clasping Rina's, tightened momentarily. "This is the path then. This is where she's been."

One of the rivulets curled up and round what looked to be a hill on the map, marked as Firle.

"X marks the spot," muttered Rina and then she looked at Aerten. "I know it's late, but—"

"Of course, we'll take my bike."

RIDING on the back of a motorbike wasn't something that Rina had ever realised that she'd thoroughly enjoy. It just hadn't occurred to her, Tunford being so small that you could walk most places. And if she really *had* to go further afield, she usually popped into her little car. But she was probably a little too overwrought to drive herself, and Aerten had offered, so when they'd walked back to the Freed Hunt's house from the library, and Aerten had grabbed a spare helmet, she suddenly realised what it all entailed.

She'd looked at the bike with a little trepidation; she hadn't straddled something that big in quite some time, but she found that sitting behind Aerten, and holding onto her solid, comforting figure, was rather satisfying.

She was even wearing a leather jacket, which seemed like the sort of thing one should do when riding a motorbike.

But the actual experience of riding along down winding lanes was enchanting.

The night sky was a deep deep indigo and it blanketed the countryside, broken up only by the light of faraway stars. There was an abiding silence that felt heavy, even with the roar of the bike cutting through it, and once more Rina felt as if the two of them were in their own tiny capsule. Them against the world. Against time.

And even in the darkness she could feel the comfort of the South Downs.

Kenna talked about it sometimes, about how the magic that dwelled in the fields had a life of its own; how it was through borrowing energy from the sky and the sea and the earth that she was able to shift forms. And ever since she'd explained it like that, the Downs had felt more alive to Rina. Rather like a kindly great aunt who takes a vague interest in the little people running around by their feet, but whose memory is so full of life and time that they can't remember all the tiny details of their lives.

It felt that way now, almost as if the fields themselves were lending speed to the bike and aiding them in their journey.

Rina had an overwhelming urge to thank them, all of a sudden. Perhaps once Sandro was found she'd set up a standing order to a conservation charity. A little thank you to all that energy that was out there.

She tapped Aerten's shoulder as they came up to the turning for Firle, and they turned off, before turning off again onto another road that was far less kempt. Driving past quiet cottages and small houses before just a long winding stretch of road that took them up and up and up.

This time, the feeling of the hills being alive wasn't just a feeling, it was a certainty. She could feel life, muted, but tangible somewhere within the mound of grass and earth and soil. The barrows, calling to her. Her brother. He was here.

THEY PULLED over onto the gravel parking at the side of the road, and Aerten had to steady the bike as Rina clamboured off it.

Aerten would have been lying if she said that she wasn't a little bit concerned about their next steps. Say they found Rina's brother. What next? Would Andraste be there too?

The wind whistling through the dark suddenly felt very cold indeed.

In the aftermath of that final battle, Brianne and she had looked for the goddess amongst the carnage, the piles of broken bodies, and found her nowhere. That had hit Bri harder than it had hit Aerten. After all they'd been through in the aftermath of their father's death – a broken treaty, their birthright stolen, the violence, the humiliation – it hadn't come as a huge surprise to Aerten when even the goddess that they'd worshipped abandoned them. But Bri, her sister? Bri had spent years working with Andraste in ways that Aerten never had, and this final betrayal had been too much for her. Even as a member of the Hunt, her heart had never been in it.

She stumbled for a moment on a pebble, remembering.

When they'd been made members of the Hunt, it had been enough for a while. She had wanted to live. To watch over the land that was hers by birth, and to watch those who came after her. But Bri had spent those first few years in a near trance. Calling and calling out to the goddess who'd left them all behind. There'd been days when she'd wanted to take her sister in her hands and shake her until she understood that this was it for them. That they were on their own and all they truly had left were each other, and the Hunt.

But that understanding never came.

She tasted salt on her lips and realised that she was crying.

The anger that usually followed the tears, loomed forth, because she really was angry. Furious with her sister for that half-whispered goodbye, and that look of peace in her eyes as Bri let herself fall off her horse and disintegrate into dust the moment she touched the ground.

Brianne had left her here.

Left her the only woman in a troop of men who didn't understand, couldn't understand, what it was like to live with those memories. That betrayal.

Aerten looked over to where Rina had begun to determinedly stride up the hillside. She would help her find her brother, and then she would find Andraste, and destroy her for the destruction she'd wrought in her absence. For her mother's death. For Brianne's suicide. The bitch would pay.

CHAPTER SIX

INTERLUDE

BENEATH THE EARTH, Alessandro Baroni waited. He wasn't entirely certain exactly what he was waiting for, but he knew it was something. Something or someone. And they would come and take him out of this hole in the ground, in which he had been buried.

And when he said he knew, he *knew*. In that weird way that his sister knew who it was, a split second before the phone rang; or the way in which his Nanna knew to hold out a hand to catch a spoon before it hit the ground.

So yes, whilst being buried alive wasn't an experience that he'd be recommending, after the initial shock and fear he'd managed to calm himself and found that sitting with your thoughts wasn't entirely bad. Not as good as video games or Jessie in his English class, but not bad at all.

And those thoughts had turned, perhaps a little surprisingly, to his family. All the time in the world, and all he could think of was them. Loud, chaotic, always interfering and poking and prodding with "Sandro, do you need help with your homework?" and "Sandro, you rat, stop mucking about with my Spotify preferences" and "Sandro, come eat something, for fuck's sake!"

Rina and Bianca were annoying – a big sister's prerogative, Bee always said – but in this moment in the dark, he'd have given almost anything to have one of them to talk to. To wind him up, or tease him about his crushes, or just to tell him that it was going to be okay.

The soil above him started to shake, and he turned his head to the side, so it wouldn't get in his eyes or up his nose, and then his sister, his quietly nerdy older sister, looking more dishevelled than he thought he'd ever seen her, was reaching down to pull him out and she was crying and laughing and all he could say was, "Took you long enough."

CHAPTER SEVEN

IT HAD TAKEN them a startlingly short amount of time to find Sandro. Unnervingly so, because Aerten was certain that it really shouldn't have been that easy. Nothing was ever that easy. Especially when the Gods were involved.

But Rina was laughing and hugging her brother and trying to work out how they were going to get the three of them back to what Sandro sardonically called 'Baroni Centrale' and she just didn't have the heart to tell her that she should probably prepare for a second offensive. That goddesses never gave up that easily.

Instead, she'd filled the hole back in that they'd dug him out of – the very conveniently placed spade left defiantly on top – and had waited for Rina and Sandro to stop talking. She was waiting a while. There were also phone calls and what sounded like a million crying relatives on the other end of the line, and then the rest of Rina's family just appeared.

Aerten had absolutely no idea how they'd all gotten there so damn quickly, but somehow they had and they were *all* there. Siblings and parents and cousins who'd surrounded

Sandro with kisses and hugs, to the fourteen year old's embarrassment, before descending upon Rina, and then, to her growing alarm, turned towards Aerten herself.

"Rina! Are you not going to introduce us?"

Aerten felt the urge to scuff her feet and hide her face, but hidden by the dusk of midnight, she settled at smiled in the general direction of someone that she assumed was Rina's mother. "I'm Aerten, Mrs Baroni."

"Angelina, I insist! Thank you so much for helping find our little Sandro."

There was a muttering from behind her that made it sound like little Sandro was not the biggest fan of that particular turn of phrase.

"Rina's a good friend; I was just happy I could help."

"Well, lunch, tomorrow, at ours. Rina will pick you up." And then they were gone and Aerten was left feeling like she'd been slightly bulldozed.

"My family are a lot." There was a light in Rina's voice that Aerten hadn't quite heard before, and she wanted to put it there over and over again. "They're a little wild and they're never quiet, but they're good people and they love me."

"I can tell." And she could. There was a warmth that rolled off them all and she was surprised that she hadn't been physically enveloped when they'd arrived. "They seem nice, but lunch seems like it will be a family thing."

It was still dark, so she didn't so much see Rina come stand next to her as much as she felt her hand slip into hers. "It's Sunday lunch so anyone can come if they've an invitation. And you helped me find Sandro, so please. Come to lunch with my family."

🧁

AERTEN HAD INSISTED on driving Rina all the way home, even though she'd pointed out that her car was parked at the Hunt's house.

When they arrived, Aerten had turned the bike off before they dismounted, so that she could walk Rina all the way to the front door of her ground floor flat.

"We haven't quite faced down Andraste yet, but we did rescue my brother. And you did say that I could get a kiss whenever I wanted so…" Rina let her voice trail off and grinned cheekily up at Aerten. "…kiss please?"

She expected a similar kiss to the one at the library, but there'd been something that had flared in Aerten's eyes at Rina's teasing words, and she was delighted when Aerten had grabbed the front of her hoodie and pulled her roughly towards her with something akin to a growl in the back of her throat.

"I like it when you say please," she murmured before plundering Rina's mouth in a manner that made her legs go weak and her pussy clench. Rina let herself melt beneath the other woman's mouth, running her own hands up to tangle in the redhead's hair and tug. That seemed to enflame Aerten's passion further and Rina made a mental note then and there to make a list of all the things that enflamed Aerten's passion, because when it resulted in her kissing Rina's neck just like that, fuck—

All coherent thoughts seemed to float away and Rina pulled the other woman closer to her. "Please."

"Please what, serch?" murmured Aerten, nipping at that place on Rina's neck that always made her head spin.

"Please stay."

Aerten pulled back and looked searchingly at Rina, who ducked her head to hide the traitorous blush that she could feel staining her cheeks.

"Stay?"

"We don't have to do *that*, but it's been a whole evening and I'd like to fall asleep knowing that someone else was there. Well, that *you* were there." It was true. Rina would happily beg Aerten for kisses all night long, but it was more than that. She wanted to curl up against her, and fall asleep in her arms. Craved it in a way that she hadn't with anyone else in a very long time.

"I would like that very much." Her words made Rina let out a breath that she didn't know that she'd been holding.

"Okay, cool, yes." She turned to unlock the door, tumbled inside and turned the light on. Suddenly awkward again, she started to the kitchen with the intention of putting the kettle on before Aerten's hand on her wrist halted her. "Is everything okay?"

"Everything is just fine." The words, murmured in her ear, were a caress that made Rina shiver. "I would just like you to say please for me a few more times."

"Oh?"

Aerten backed Rina up against her hallway wall, her eyes darkened with desire, "Yes, serch. I want you to say please in that oh so pretty way that you do."

"Please what?" the challenge in Rina's voice was a little cautious, uncertain of its reception.

She shouldn't have worried because Aerten grinned at the mischievous retort. "Now that is up to you, serch."

"Fine," Rina rolled her eyes, secretly delighted. "Please Aerten, please kiss me."

"And?"

Her nipples tightened before words came tumbling out, a mix of embarrassment and excitement and lust. "Please kiss me til my head spins. Please kiss and bite my neck, like you did just now only *more*, I want more please. I want to lose my mind and to keen and moan and cry out for you and to please you over and over and then I want to fall asleep curled up in your arms, with you stroking my hair please please please."

It wasn't often that Rina spoke her desires out loud like that, and if she did, they were usually far more collected and basically a statement of fact, rather than the desperate keening and pleading that had just fallen from her lips. She'd never begged for anything in her life.

It turned out that begging made her wet.

She had a feeling that her begging had a similar impact on Aerten because the other woman's mouth came down hard upon hers and then they were stumbling across the room until the back of Rina's knees hit the arm of her couch and she went tumbling backwards.

RINA LAY on her back on the sofa, looking up at Aerten and Aerten thought that she might just expire. The flushed face, those dazed eyes, and the adorable way in which she bit her lip when she was aroused.

It was delicious.

Rina was delicious, and Aerten was intent on eating her all up.

She shed her top as she climbed on top of Rina, straddling her thighs and running her hands up under the hoodie. "My turn to say please," she whispered, and Rina discarded the garment eagerly, sitting up to capture Aerten's lips with hers. Underneath she wore a white – brassiere, Aerten believed the term was – but even through the gossamer thin lace she could see where Rina's nipples had pebbled and she couldn't help but dip her mouth to one before hovering, waiting.

"What are you waiting for?" asked Rina, trying to arch up to her mouth.

"You know what."

"Oh come on Aerten, *please*."

"Oh if I must." But she was laughing even as she moved aside the lace to tug the nipple into her mouth. The brunette was just so damn responsive. She could spend all day listening to those darling little sighs and moan and each 'please' that she uttered.

There was something about that word on Rina's lips that drove Aerten wild. It made her want to taste every inch of her skin until Rina was so desperate that she'd beg over and over and over. And she wanted, she *needed*, to make Rina come apart.

She slipped a hand down between them and there were a few moments of some cursing as Rina tried to shimmy out of her jeans. Leaning back on her heels, she started to laugh as the attempts got more and more wild until Rina just fell off the sofa with a "fuck!" And then Aerten was on her knees next to her, kissing her all better.

The battle with the jeans continued, Rina getting up and wriggling out of them in a manner that was more than a little bewitching, until a delightfully lacy *thing* was revealed. A lacy thing which was so wet she could see the distinct shape of lips beneath the material.

In that moment, Aerten had grabbed onto Rina's lace-covered arse with both hands and nosed at that heavenly join between her legs. Once, twice and then "Oh for fuck's sake, fine Aerten, please. Please lick me!"

She ran her hands up the inside of Rina's legs and in one sharp tug, tore the material in two. "I'll replace it," she murmured.

"I don't care," answered Rina before running her hands through Aerten's hair and nudging her closer to her quim.

With one finger, she skimmed her touch across Rina's clit, before running across her lips, marvelling at how plump and pink and ready she was. And then, as Rina bucked against Aerten's fingers, she leaned forward to lap at the nub.

Rina swore.

Aerten liked it when Rina swore. It was beyond cute. She determined to make her swear again. Another lick, another curse, and then, drunk on desire and longing and Rina's taste, she dove in.

She alternated between thrumming fingers across Rina's clit and sliding them inside her slickness, all the while licking and lapping at her core. This was, she decided, her happy place. In between Rina's legs, tasting her desire, and hearing the sweetest mewls and moans emanating from the brunette.

"Oh my, just there, oh please Aerten, please please please make me-" Rina's voice cut off as she came, her cunt spasming around Aerten's fingers in a most satisfactory manner.

She withdrew her fingers, licked off the remainder of Rina's juices, and then softly pushed her back onto the sofa so that Rina sat down, before Aerten clambered up in a rather ungainly fashion to join her.

As much as the pleading had been delightful, the cuddling that followed was even more satisfying. As she pulled Rina close, the other woman pretty much wound herself round Aerten, nudging at her hand with silky brown hair until Aerten began to stroke.

Sex was great; making this pretty lass come was wonderful; but this? Quiet snuggles and hair strokes? It calmed a part of Aerten's soul that she hadn't realised needed calming. Something about running her fingers through Rina's hair as she settled in Aerten's lap, the repetition of the small movement simple and quiet, let a weight fall from Aerten. This moment was theirs. She didn't have to think about anyone or anything else, but just focus on the woman who'd put herself literally into Aerten's hands. And it was wonderful.

CHAPTER EIGHT

AT SOME POINT after that rather marvellous orgasm, Rina had dragged Aerten into her bedroom. It was a small room, the whole flat being more cosy than expansive, but it was cute and tidy and decorated in a pale blue that never failed to put Rina at ease.

She'd expected, had *wanted*, to reciprocate, but Aerten had murmured something about sleep and tomorrow morning, and instead they'd snuggled, Rina the little spoon to Aerten's big, and fallen asleep together quite easily.

It had been a long time since Rina had slept with someone, and even longer since she'd actually had someone in her bed. It was so personal, having someone inside her house, inside her own space. Sex and orgasms didn't always mean a relationship, and Rina knew that she didn't usually want anyone in her bed unless she knew it was going somewhere, which made her decision the previous night to invite Aerten in a little odd.

She turned her head to sneak a peek at the other sleeping woman. There was a curl of red hair that had fallen across a cheek dotted with freckles, and Rina had a sudden urge to dot-to-dot across them with her fingers.

Aerten was beautiful and strong and surprisingly sweet, but probably wouldn't appreciate getting woken up by having a finger poked in her face.

Sliding out of bed, Rina slipped on the dressing gown that was hung up behind the door, and tiptoed her way to the kitchen.

Coffee. She needed coffee.

Once the machine was merrily making the comforting sounds that preceded a really decent cup of black coffee, coffee that Rina needed in order to function, she slipped onto the stool by the breakfast bar that split her kitchen from the living room.

So. What did it mean?

She could have chalked it up to the adrenaline after finding Sandro, but that seemed like a cop out. The honest truth was that she liked Aerten. A lot. And also, that Aerten was fucking hot.

Rina felt herself flush at the remembrance of all the begging that she'd done the previous night. The begging and the pleading and how very very hot it had made her; hot and slick and…

The machine beeped at just the right moment and managed to divert Rina's attention. Because thinking on *that* would result in very little getting done that day at all.

She grabbed her phone to check the time as she sipped the dark elixir. Only 11 am. Just enough time for a hot shower – in more than one sense of the word – before they had to leave for lunch. But when she swivelled on the stool to head back and wake Aerten up, the best way she knew how, there was someone standing in front of her.

Rina almost threw coffee in Andraste's face. The only

thing that stopped her was the fact that it would probably ruin her carpet, and she'd only had it refitted recently.

"What," she asked icily, "the *fuck* are you doing in my home?"

"What do you think?" asked the goddess.

Standing up, she paused to put her coffee down before getting right up in the goddess' face. "I think," she said, her words clipped and her tone getting colder by the minute, "that you have made a mistake coming here."

The audacity of the laugh that followed had Rina grabbing Andraste by the hair and slamming her cheek down onto the breakfast bar. "You. Took. My. Brother."

There was a silence before Andraste ground out. *"And yet I didn't hurt him. I merely demonstrated that cooperating with me would be a good idea."*

Tightening her fist in the red hair, Rina was briefly tempted to smash Andraste's face against the bar again and again. In fact, she almost did until she noticed the smirk on the goddess' face and found herself letting go, pushing away and swiftly walking round so she stood with the breakfast bar between them. A barrier.

"What-what was that? What did you just do to me?"

Andraste gave an amused snort. *"I didn't do anything. That was all you. Well, mostly you."*

"Mostly?"

"I am a warrior goddess. The warrior goddess. Your anger fed off that. Besides," she continued, *"I like anger. It's a healthy emotion to feel, and when you offer that kind of energy up to me, it's the best possible freolac – oblation – you can give me."*

Rina felt her temper rise again and shoved it back down unceremoniously. "I'm not making any kind of an offering to you. I don't want anything to do with you. And I certainly don't want you feeding off my energy."

Andraste rolled her eyes, an action that seemed startlingly

modern when Rina considering the pelt adorning the goddess' shoulders and the woad adorning her face. *"Mortals. Always so stubborn. I suppose I shall give you some time then, to consider exactly all you have to lose if you persist in defying me."*

"Rina? Serch? Is everything well?"

In films, there's that slow motion moment which always seems ridiculously over the top, where everything centres in on one single movement. It seemed less ridiculous to Rina in real life, faced with the prospect of Aerten coming face to face with the figure of her nightmares. Rina wasn't entirely certain what would happen if the two were in the same room as each other, but she imagined that it wouldn't be good, and she wasn't prepared for Aerten to deal with the shock of seeing the goddess without sufficient warning.

"Fine, yes, whatever," she hissed at goddess. "Just go."

"You dare-"

"Rina?" Aerten rounded the corner and froze. "What the fuck-" Rina saw panic flit cross the redhead's face and she slipped round the breakfast bar to go stand next to her.

"It turns out," she said in the fakest cheerful voice she'd ever used, "that we have a visitor this morning."

There was a deathly silence and she felt Aerten's shoulders stiffen even more, her fist clenching and clenching beneath Rina's hand.

Okay. So no fighting yet.

But when she looked over at the goddess, the deity was so pale she almost seemed translucent, her mouth half open in shock. *"Brianne?"*

HEARING her sister's name shredded any kind of self-control that Aerten had been clinging on to. She launched herself across the room, grabbing Andraste by the pelt and shoving her up against the wall.

"You dare say her name? You whom caused her death? Who caused all of our deaths?" She shook the goddess once, twice, thrice, slamming the back of the goddess' head against some cabinet with each movement, and would have continued if it hadn't been for the fact that Andraste was not fighting back.

Andraste always fought back.

She let go and stalked across to the other side of the room, staring out the window and seeing nothing. The silence in the room was heavy, and she knew that only she could break it. The words, when they came, were clipped. Bitter. "What do you want, Andraste?"

The answer was quiet, each word a bite. *"Want? I want more things that you could conceive. But I'll start with my oracle."*

That made Aerten turn around "You shall not have her; I will not allow you."

"Ahem."

They both whirled on Rina, who raised an eyebrow. She looked a little pissed off. With both of them. "I'd like to point out that I am not some *thing* to be argued over. I am a person with my own very definitive opinions about what I shall or shall not be doing. And oracling is not on the agenda for today thank you very much. But," here she shot a look at Aerten, "'You shall not have her'? Really?! That's what you go with?"

There was a pause in which Aerten realised that the question had not been hypothetical. "Oh. Should I not have?"

Rina strode across the room in as large steps as her shorter legs could manage, until she was standing in front of Aerten, folding her arms and furrowing her brow. "Is this some kind of alpha warrior woman thing? Over-protective girlfriend mode or something?"

Aerten blinked a few times.

She could see Andraste over Rina's shoulder. The goddess moved to sit atop a tall stool and was smirking – *smirking* – at Aerten.

"I…" she wasn't sure exactly what it was that Rina wanted to hear, but she would give it a good go. "I was trying to help…?"

The brunette raised her hands to the sky and threw them down again in one swift movement, before going on her tiptoes to kiss Aerten hard. "That's very sweet, but next time please ask. I don't need rescuing."

"Well actually-"

"Shut it." Her voice was suddenly frosty as she rounded on the goddess and Aerten was relieved that she'd only gotten a mild rebuke. She never wanted to hear Rina use that tone with her. It was more than a little scary. "I'm done with you today. I'm still pissed off and all you're doing is stopping me from doing the things I want to do. I don't like that. So kindly fuck off."

And to Aerten's astonishment, the goddess did. One moment she was there, and the next she was nowhere to be seen.

That had all happened rather quickly, and as quickly as it had risen, her rage drained away and she felt herself stagger slightly. Reaching out, she grabbed the corner of the couch and sat down before she fell down. Because no one liked to fall over in front of a paramour.

"Are you okay?" The earnest look on Rina's face almost had her reaching for a lie, but she took a breath and paused. Shrugged.

"What do you need? Water? Some sugar? I think I've got some pastries in the cupboard somewhere-" and the babbling faded as Aerten tugged at Rina's hand.

Just the once.

Asking for help this one time wasn't a big deal, right? It was practically an exchange of favours – she'd helped Rina find her brother and now Rina was... Rina was...

Rina was sitting down next to her, and pulling her close until Aerten's head rested upon those wonderful breasts. Any other time they'd have provided the most delicious distraction, but right now they were comfort.

Two arms encircled her, pulling her close, and she felt Rina tuck her chin so that it fit over Aerten's head.

Oh. Alright. Just this once.

CHAPTER NINE

THEY SAT like that for some time, so quiet that Rina wasn't entirely certain whether or not Aerten had gone to sleep. It was nice. Peaceful. Especially in the aftermath of that disastrous encounter with Andraste.

She probably should have found it quite scary, the way in which Aerten had moved with such speed to violence, but she didn't. Nothing Aerten did scared her, Rina realised. That was quite a nice realisation. It wasn't a red flag, it was just a different way of processing, as had been the whole staking her ground over Rina the oracle thing.

That was kind of adorable, especially when Aerten had looked so confused and a little panicked at the idea that she'd done something wrong. Rina had wanted to kiss that frown away, had done so in fact, and seemed to have been rewarded with this moment of vulnerability.

Aerten lifted her head and smiled, this sweet quiet smile that made Rina want to do a dance. "Thank you."

"You're so welcome."

"Should we not prepare though?"

"Prepare?"

"For lunch with your family?"

"Oh *fuck!*" She threw a glance at the clock on the wall. "*Crap.* Are you sure you want to..."

Aerten nodded.

"As long as you're sure; I'll grab you a towel, but it'll have to be an in and out shower and then we'll have to head out."

Aerten allowed herself to be bustled into the bathroom as Rina tried very very hard not to think about the redhead's body all soaped up and bewailed her thwarted plans for a joint shower. She didn't even allow herself a moment to linger over the vision that was damp Aerten walking through her living room, wrapped in a towel, before she dove into a very cold shower.

It would not be good to be late for lunch; it'd invite way too many questions from her siblings about exactly *why* they were late, and a Look from her mother. Rina might have her librarian voice, but nothing was comparable to her mother's Look.

Sunday lunch at the Baronis' was a bit of an event. Whenever she'd brought someone along – both Arlee and Kenna had been staples at the Baroni table over the last few years – they usually emerged shellshocked, and so full that they were barely able to walk. Just as it should be. But as for partners...

Her sister Bianca had brought a few of her boyfriends round, but Rina had never really bothered bring any of the women she'd dated home. None of them had seemed permanent enough to entrust with an invitation to Sunday lunch and yet it felt that Aerten, a woman she'd known for merely weeks, should come with her.

And yes, the invitation hadn't been as her girlfriend – it had been as dual saviour of Sandro – but... Rina stopped, and looked over at Aerten as she put her shoes on.

"Aerten?"

"Yes serch?"

"Um…what is…*this*?"

The other woman looked over at her and smiled this smile that made Rina's heart almost stop in her chest. "Well, you called me your overprotective girlfriend."

"Oh. Shit. Yes. Yes, I did." That was very true, even if it had been in the heat of the moment and not as talked through and consented to as Rina would have liked. "You're okay with that?"

"Rina, serch," Aerten straightened up and stepped so close that Rina could have counted each individual eyelash. Her hands moved to cup Rina's face, and Rina found her pulse beating that much faster. "I do indeed feel a little overprotective of you, of that there can be no doubt."

"But the girlfriend bit…"

"'The girlfriend bit'," the woman laughed and Rina felt that all the way down to her toes. "Serch, I would not have pleasured you the way that I had, if I hadn't had *intentions*."

Intentions. The word stole Rina's breath and she couldn't find it in her to resent the thief for it. Intentions meant, well, *intentions*. "Oh." She breathed it out and felt herself flush.

"I believe that I should speak to you about such intentions – Arlee had words with us all about making assumptions with paramours – and as you asked the question…"

"I-" Rina cleared her throat as Aerten's thumb caressed her cheek. "I would be open to a conversation about intentions."

The intensity in Aerten's eyes made Rina melt. She was gooey. And puddly. And possibly pretty fucking wet. "Well, I intend to court you. I'm aware that we have already-" Here Aerten broke off and a small, self-satisfied grin crept across her face. "-yes… And I am definitely intent on more of *that*. But also, I would like to get to know, your friends, your family, your world. I want to see if I could be part of it. Would that be acceptable?"

Would that be acceptable?! The only reason Rina was not jumping Aerten right now, was the fact that they were running dangerously late for Sunday lunch. "That would be acceptable." And then the softest kiss was butterflying her lips.

SUNDAY LUNCH WAS TERRIFYING.

Aerten had faced down hordes of Roman soldiers from her chariot, seen her world fall apart, and spent centuries stuck behind the Veil. But nothing quite compared to Sunday lunch.

Rina had tried to reassure her before they'd arrived. "So there are two things really: firstly, we're pretty loud. And by pretty loud, I mean that there's usually five conversations happening at the same time. Arlee calls it cultural chaos. And my family's Italian, which means that we've Roman roots." At that she shot a look at Aerten. "Will you be okay?"

Aerten had heard the unspoken words there; and resolved to keep her emotions firmly under control if she heard the accented lilt that sometimes haunted her dreams. She'd be fine. Completely. This was easy.

That was a lie.

There was nothing easy about the – how had Rina put it? – cultural chaos of her family's meal.

It had begun when Rina's mother had enveloped Aerten in a hug. She wasn't averse to people touching her – a pat on the shoulder in solidarity from one of the Hunt, the clasping of hands at greeting, and of course kisses from Rina – but this was a whole new level of welcome.

She stood there, her body wooden in the hug, not knowing whether to relax into it, or to just continue standing there, until she saw Rina's mortified face over her mother's shoulder. That made a gurgle of laughter come curling up to her lips and she repressed it quickly before it could escape.

"Mum!"

"Che cosa?" Letting go, Angelina Baroni looked confused.

Rina grabbed Aerten's hand and pulled her into her side, "Let's not completely overwhelm Aerten, okay? It's her first time eating with an Italian family and that's going to be trial enough for her!"

"Trial seems a little like an exaggeration," Aerten interjected. "Thank you so much for inviting me Angelina; I'm looking forward to lunch."

"Of course! After helping found our little Sandro, it's the least we could do!"

And then she was being dragged out into the back garden where the Baronis seemed to be taking advantage of the weather's clemency to eat outside.

There were a lot of people there, and it felt like a wall of noise hit her when Aerten stepped outside. Snippets of multiple conversations, all of which seemed rather heated, swept over her and she blinked several times in succession.

"Hey." A dark-haired woman, who looked a little like Rina, offered her a beer. "I'm Bianca, Rina's sister. The sibling who didn't get themselves buried alive." Sandro, who was passing, swiped at her and she dodged neatly. "Why don't you come grab a seat? That way people can come to you, and it's not so much that way – or so I've been told."

Aerten allowed herself to be led to a seat, and then Rina, with a rather awkward kiss on the cheek, excused herself to pop and say hi to her grandparents. It warmed her, seeing how nervous her lass was with showing that affection in front of her whole family but doing it anyway. It was very sweet. Bianca threw herself into the seat next to Aerten and grinned. "Rina will do the whole running around, talking to all the family thing for a little bit before she sits back down, but I texted her earlier and told her I'd keep an eye out for you before the masses descend. So. You shagging my sister?"

There was a long pause in which Aerten very deliberately did not meet Bianca's eyes, and instead took a swig of her beer.

"Ah, no comment? You guys dating then?"

From what she'd managed to glean over the last few weeks of bouncing work, dating was a concept akin to courtship so she nodded, suddenly cognisant of the fact that this was some kind of interrogation. "I care for your sister very much," she said, determined not to be ridden roughshod. "She is kind and beautiful and quieter than the rest of your family seems to be."

That made Bianca laugh and Aerten's shoulders untensed. "Fair enough, we're definitely a pretty rowdy bunch. Rina would probably kill me if she guessed I was quizzing you about your relationship, so how about we switch to safer topics. What do you do?"

Well, thought Aerten, *I was originally the heir to a kingdom, and then when that was stolen from me, became a warrior, saw my army and family slaughtered, and then was trapped in the Wild Hunt for two millennia.* Out loud she said, "I work in security; do some work as a bouncer in Brighton and for Tegan at the Golden Martlet."

"That's a pretty intense role for a woman; anyone give you any grief?"

"Hen parties are the *worst*," she said with feeling, and by Bianca's answering chuckle, that seemed to be an appropriate answer. "How about you?"

"Me? I work in our restaurant as a chef – got today off on

Mum's orders though. And I'm heading out to Italy in a few months, to do a speciality course in the region us Baronis come from."

Rina flopped down in the chair on the other side of Aerten and pulled a face at Bianca. "Stop hogging my girl; everyone wants to meet her."

"They do?" Her heart sped up a little in panic, but Rina's hand atop hers calmed her down and she took some small calming breaths. Perhaps it was unsurprising that an experience like this was a little destabilising. For so long it had just been her and the Hunt, and yes, they'd expanded that circle out a little to include Rina, Arlee and Kenna, but that was still only a handful of people. She could count at least twelve other people in the garden.

But when Rina smiled at her, there was understanding along with warmth. "I know there's quite a lot of us, but everyone's super friendly, and once we start eating, you'll be able to just experience it all."

CHAPTER TEN

HER FAMILY WERE BEHAVING THEMSELVES. That was a relief, at least. She'd seen panic flash across Aerten's face more than once, and was relieved that Bianca had offered to sit on one side of her, and Sandro across the table, so that there was some semblance of normality.

Or so she thought until the food came out.

This was not a normal Sunday lunch. Normal Sunday lunch usually meant a roast dinner with an Italian twist. There was no Sunday lunch in sight.

She shot an accusatory look at Bianca, who just shrugged and spooned more food onto her plate.

Her mum had done a proper four course spread. Gnoccho fritto and prosciutto for antipasti: fluffy deep-fried pasta dough clouds, with delicious salty cured meat. Tortellini en brodo for primo, which she just knew that Bianca must have made up that morning in the restaurant's kitchen, because it had that distinct full flavour that made her tastebuds water. And then steak with salad for secondi.

Luckily Aerten didn't seem to realise that this wasn't quite the norm for Sunday lunch. She took everything at face value, having hearty portions of each course and making all of the right delighted noises whilst eating. Her mother was beaming and even Bianca had a self-satisfied grin when Aerten pronounced the tortellini "perfection!"

She'd looked a little stunned when Rina's cousins had started arguing about music in the usual Baroni manner – which meant very loudly and seemingly aggressively – but seemed to shake it off in favour of diving into some stewed apples and ice cream.

As Rina helped clear the plates, her quiet dad had pulled her to one side and just nodded and smiled. "She's nice, Rina."

She was grateful that most of the family had just taken Aerten's presence as granted, and hadn't asked too many questions, although the knowing looks implied that they all knew that she was a girlfriend of sorts. It was lovely how her family took her sexuality in their stride, just as they had with her cousins; no pauses in conversation when she held Aerten's hand or kissed her cheek, but rather smiles that said that they were happy for her.

Technically Aerten had been invited because of Sandro, but it was pretty clear to everyone that they'd come together. As in *together* together.

Rina had never done that before.

And yet here Aerten was, sat in the midst of the wildness that was her family, eating and trying ever so hard to keep up with the multiple conversations that were being directed at her all at once. Every now and then she looked around for Rina, as if reassuring herself that she hadn't been abandoned to the cultural chaos, and each time their eyes met, Aerten just smiled. It was this secret smile, not in that no one else saw it, but in that it held secret promises of laughter and kisses and making Rina plead for pleasure all over again.

In this moment, surrounded by the people that she loved

and with a woman that she was beginning to think that, one day, she might love, Rina could forget the threat that hovered over them. Almost. She looked across as where Sandro was sat quietly. Her brother never did *anything* quietly. She kicked him under the table and then nodded towards the kitchen door, and he nodded at her.

They cleared plates, as an excuse, and then, when they'd managed to get some distance from the rest of the family, she sighed. "Are you okay?"

He nodded again. "It's okay sis, I knew you were coming."

"I know, but–"

"No, as in I *knew* knew."

She paused, taking that in. "Oh."

"So I'm okay, though I'd rather not get buried alive again. Not exactly a pleasant experience."

Looking at him, Rina realised that he thought he was telling the truth. There might have been panic at first, but right now he genuinely wasn't too upset about the whole thing. "You'll do therapy though?"

He barked a laugh, "Like I have a choice."

"Yeah." There was a silence. Rina hadn't realised quite how much she'd been blaming herself for what had happened until now; relief flooded her and she sighed, releasing with it some of her guilt. "So the woman who took you…"

Sandro grabbed a chair and sat down. "You want a description for the police? Because I'm not sure she… I'm not sure that she's the kind of person a police cell could hold. I know that sounds ridiculous," he rushed on, before she could speak, "But I know it, just as I knew that you were going to find me. Rina, she…she just *appeared*, face all painted blue, looking like something out of a story and then we were on the hillside and I couldn't move, I couldn't run away, I was just stuck there whilst she dug a hole and threw me in."

She was suddenly infused with a rage so strong that it

almost overwhelmed her. No matter what she had done or indeed refused to do, Andraste should have kept her family out of this. Sandro had nothing to do with any of this, and he'd been through an ordeal that she realised – even if he didn't – had somewhat traumatised him. For her active, ever-moving brother to have to be forced to stay still, against his will, she couldn't imagine the damage that it would have done.

Her fist clenched as if of its own accord, and when she felt the bite of her own nails against her skin she almost jumped, and let her hands fall limply to her sides. Deep breaths, pulling herself back from that edge before she let her anger consume her.

Sitting down heavily on the other kitchen chair, she ran her hand across her face. "I'm sorry, Sandro. I didn't know that she'd do that."

Rina couldn't read the look that he shot her, but his silence felt damning.

"Seriously, I had no idea–" A foot kicked gently at her leg.

"Shut up. It's not your fault. How could you possibly have known?" Sandro was young, but his fierceness imbued his every word. "I don't know how to stop her from grabbing anyone else though."

"Leave that with me." Standing up, Rina smiled tiredly at her brother. "That's my job to sort out."

AERTEN WASN'T sure where Rina and her brother had disappeared off to, but she was going to have to have words with her serch about abandoning her to the tender mercies of her aunts and uncles. Her sister and the trio of cousins, Silvana, Celestia and Liliana, who sat nearby, all interjected fairly regularly, in an attempt to try and stem the waves of questions that Aerten wasn't always entirely sure how to answer. She'd worked out that distracting Rina's elder family members with talk of food seemed to work, however, and so she'd asked what the best filling for tortellini was, and then made her escape.

Rina was stood in the kitchen with Sandro when Aerten walked in and clearly noticed the fatigue that she felt. "I'm stealing my girlfriend away," she declared, with a shy look at Aerten as she said the world girlfriend. She had to stop herself from grinning inanely back at the brunette.

There were hugs and promises of future visits and just whole lot of what she had come to realise was the Baroni standard, before they left the house.

"Was it too much? We are a whole lot sometimes."

She pondered the question for a moment, not wanting to give Rina a glib answer. "No, I don't think so. I'm not used to such chaos, of course, but that's not to say it wasn't nice. Your family are very welcoming, if inquisitive. They love you very much."

The laugh her serch gave almost burst from her, and Aerten looked at her curiously.

"Not everyone gets them," explained Rina. "And that's okay, only I couldn't, I *can't*, be with someone who doesn't get my family. Because if they don't get my family, then that's a huge part of me that they don't get either."

That made sense to Aerten. She didn't think that she could have a paramour who hated the other members of the Hunt; for all that they were strangers in some ways, they'd become a makeshift family of their own, and she knew who she was with them. "I understand."

Rina looked at her for a long time, as if searching out some truth in her eyes, before giving a short nod, and then pressing her lips against Aerten's. Dropping the bag of food that she'd been given to the floor, Aerten pulled Rina close, arms slipping around that waist until she couldn't tell where she ended and Rina began. All consuming passion was one thing, but she could lose herself for days in kisses like these; soft, delicate butterfly kisses that made her feel like she was something, someone, to be cherished.

When they broke apart, Rina smiled thoughtfully. "I'd like to take you somewhere, if you don't mind?"

Aerten would have followed her through the Veil if she'd asked.

"Would you mind taking us back to my car, and then I can drive us?"

She checked the timepiece on her arm. "I have work in a few hours at the Martlet; will we be able to return in time?"

Rina grinned and went on her tiptoes to kiss Aerten's cheek. The touch of her mouth felt almost like a claiming. "I'll drop you at work after; does that sound okay?"

"Of course."

The ride back to the Hunt's house was short, must only have been ten minutes at the most, but Aerten felt every second of them. She'd discovered this problem the night before; it was difficult to concentrate on the roads with her serch's lithe form pressed up close against her back, but Aerten had ridden into battle with arrows and swords coming in her direction. She could do this without a problem.

But by the time they dismounted, she was breathing ever so slightly faster, and she could feel her blood thudding through her veins. Rina's hair had gotten messy under the helmet, and she looked good enough to eat. It turned out that seeing her prim and proper librarian all mussed up was enough to send her pulse skyrocketing. She briefly toyed with the prospect of taking her up to bed, but then discarded it when Rina's glowing face smiled up at her, and the other woman grabbed her hand and pulled her towards the car.

Sitting in the passenger seat, with Rina driving was a somewhat unnerving experience. It wasn't just that Aerten was used to being the one in charge of her rides – horse, chariot or bike – but it was also the casualness with which Rina took to the road. It was not normal to ride in a metal box and talk as if you weren't riding a chariot of death about. She'd seen enough accidents from the other side of the Veil, to know that. And yet here her serch was, chatting away as if nothing was the matter.

When they finally pulled up by the side of the road, her palms were sweaty and she'd found herself almost petitioning for a safe journey, despite the fact that she hadn't petitioned the gods for anything in millennia. She was about to say as much, before Rina jumped out and came round to open her car door, and she saw where they were.

CHAPTER ELEVEN

THE SKY above them was a brilliant blue, but that wasn't what made Aerten stop and stare. The field before them did that.

"What do you think?" Rina's voice was quiet, and the other woman's face looked serene. "Isn't it beautiful?"

Aerten stepped out of the car, and onto the verge of the grass. "Can we…?"

Rina nodded.

And then she just started walking.

All about her were thousands and thousands of poppies, all laid out as far as the eye could see, blanketing the hillsides with perfectly bobbing red heads. As she walked, they danced about her knees, petals brushing her fingertips and she wanted to twirl on the spot and just revel in the sight. She was not usually a twirling person, before the Veil or after it, but this made her want to dance.

When she stopped, Rina walked up behind her and slipped her hand into Aerten's. "We're lucky; they'll only be here for a few more weeks." She tugged at Aerten's hand, and then pulled her down until they were both lying side by side, the red flowers kissing above their heads.

They didn't cosy up or cuddle, but just lay there, looking at the poppies, so red against the blue of the sky. The longing to twirl abated, replaced with something deeper, more solid.

This was what she wanted.

This was what had been missing.

Not loudness and hot bodies clinging to each other, skin to skin, although she'd missed that too, but this feeling was what had been missing.

She'd been so angry, so grief-stricken, for so long that Aerten had forgotten what peace felt like. And it felt like this: soft swish of the breeze through the flowers; a sky dotted with clouds that could never threaten rain; and this hand in hers, grounding her, keeping her here, keeping her present.

She shifted, and Rina pulled her close, gently coaxing her until she was curled up on her side, her head resting on her serch's arm.

"I love the poppies." Rina's voice was almost a whisper. "When I get too overwhelmed, when life stresses me out just that little bit too much, somehow there's always a poppy field for me to go lie in. As if the universe just knows that I need *something* to keep me going." She took a shuddery breath, and Aerten realised that the woman who held her was trembling. "I've lain here in sunshine and in rain, but always on my own."

Leaning up, she cupped Rina's cheek with her hand, heart aching as the woman leant into her palm, wanting to envelope her with warmth and comfort. "I wish you hadn't been on your own."

Tears sprung to Rina's eyes and she dashed them away fiercely. "If I hadn't been on my own then, this wouldn't mean so much."

The truth in the brunette's words hit Aerten hard. That

was as much a truth for herself as it was for Rina. She truly felt peace here in this moment, because it had been so disturbed for so many centuries before. This moment was all the more precious for the contrasting vision it presented against her own history.

"It is peaceful here." She knew her words didn't do justice to the enormity that she felt, but Rina nodded, and Aerten knew that she didn't have to explain, just as Rina hadn't needed to explain. They just understood each other.

WHEN RINA DROPPED Aerten off at the pub later that evening, she felt drained. She watched the other woman stride towards the door of The Martlet, pause for a moment, and then turn to give her a shy wave. She waved back and then leant back in her seat and sighed once the redhead walked into the pub.

This was a different kind of overwhelm; one that didn't call for lying in a poppy field. Grabbing her phone, she sent a gif out to Kenna and Arlee, one of a mouse hiding in a cup, and got responses almost immediately.

Kenna: Are you okay? Why are you hiding?

Arlee: Of course she's not okay – gifs instead of words?! This is a true emergency!

Kenna: Fuck. Rina. Where are you? Do you need us to come get you?

Arlee: Kenna, ditch Morcant for the evening. You're both coming to mine. I have ice cream and Netflix.

Kenna: Way ahead of you, he's been ditched. Rina, do you need me to pick you up?

Her friends were everything.

Rina: I'm in the car, I'll pick you up outside the forge K.

It was just as well that she was picking up Kenna first, she realised as the blacksmith slid into the passenger seat. She wouldn't bombard Rina with questions the way that Arlee would when they arrived at their place, so she had a slight reprieve from the overwhelm and was able to collect herself a little bit.

Of the three of them, Arlee was the only one with an actual house, though they denied that loudly. "I have a *cottage*, not a house!" they'd yell. "And it's only because of Gramps."

Arlee's grandfather had been the only person in their family to not even blink when they'd come out as non-binary, and he'd helped them buy the cottage, though it had been the biggest fixer-upper project that any of them had ever seen. But it was on the edge of Tunford, near the woods and the lake, and walking distance from the primary school, so the three years spent rewiring and tiling and painting after work and in the school holidays had been worth it.

Out of all of them, Rina was glad that Arlee had been the one to own a place first. They needed the stability, and they flung open their doors and ushered in anyone they saw struggling.

They flung the door open now, and practically dragged Rina in, before pushing her onto the sofa and dumping a ton of blankets on top of her. When she finally fought her way out from under a particularly fluffy purple throw, she found her two best friends looking at her.

"Ice cream first, or talking about it?"

"Ice cream."

But she hadn't taken more than a spoonful before she put the spoon back in the bowl and took a deep breath. If she didn't talk about it now, she knew herself well enough that it'd all come bubbling up later. "The last twenty-four hours have been *a lot*."

Arlee clambered up onto the sofa next to her, and folded their legs up underneath them. "Define a lot."

"Okay... Yesterday I was visited by a goddess in the library. Warrior goddess by the name of Andraste. Has some history with Aerten."

"Our Aerten?" Rina shot Kenna a look. Even amidst everything, she wasn't sure how she felt about anyone else claiming Aerten as their own.

"Yes. Aerten. Andraste wants me to do some oracling for her, and when I refused, she took Sandro."

That had her friends getting to their feet, and it took a good fifteen minutes of cajoling and explaining until they understood that Sandro was found and safe home again and no, they really *didn't* need to go haring off into the night to have words with a goddess who was goodness even knew where.

"Why didn't you tell us before?" asked Kenna, "You know we'd have helped look for him. I could even have asked Belisama for help"

"Well, I went where my intuition told me to go, to the Hunt." That was certainly one explanation, but the truth – that she'd wanted Aerten's strength and safety – was left lingering on the tip of her tongue.

Arlee opened their mouth, and then uncharacteristically shut it.

"What?"

"It's just, did you go to the Hunt, or did you go to Aerten?"

Kenna looked as shocked as Rina felt. "Why would she go to Aerten?"

"Yes Rina, why would you go to Aerten?"

Faced with two uncompromisingly kind stares, she sighed. "Fine, I went to Aerten. I don't know why, I just... She looked after me in the battle. So I figured she'd look after me now."

"And did she?" asked Kenna.

Rina couldn't help the blush the spread across her face.

"*Oh*," said Arlee. "She 'looked after you'."

Taking a big spoon of ice cream, Rina tried to distract herself from their questions with some self-imposed brain freeze. It didn't work. She explained about taking Aerten to Sunday lunch and the poppy field and she swore Arlee's mouth literally dropped open.

"So, what's the problem then?" asked Kenna gently. "None of that seems to warrant a timid mouse gif."

Rina was wondering that herself. It had been a kneejerk reaction, to send that message, but she wasn't sure why. She liked Aerten, they'd had great sex, she'd gotten along with Rina's family, and they'd shared an emotional moment in the field. The stress of what had happened to her brother aside, there was no reason why she should be feeling this overwhelmed right now.

"Vulnerability."

"Huh?" Both Rina and Kenna looked at Arlee.

"Vulnerability. Rina, I love you hun, but you're not exactly the most open person in the world. You let us in a little, your family a little, but it's always just a little. A tiny bit here and there. You're far more comfortable with plans and research and organising things, so you can keep everything nice and tidy. Even during the battle, you were focused on the practicalities of freeing the Hunt." They reached out and took Rina's hand in theirs. "I'm not saying this to be mean lovey, but it makes perfect sense why you're exhausted after allowing Aerten to see you at your most vulnerable. You're not used to processing all of those kinds of emotions."

Rina blinked several times. That all seemed…plausible. Her fingers itched to find a book, to get researching, and Arlee squeezed her hand tight.

"Nope, no research about vulnerability. What you need is

safety. And you're in luck because it's a bank holiday tomorrow, so I don't have to be anywhere. We're going to cuddle puddle under these blankets, fall asleep whilst watching trash tv, and then sleep in tomorrow morning."

"But…"

"No buts," said Kenna gently, shifting so that she flanked Rina on the other side. "Unless we're watching something particularly salacious."

"I could go for salacious," said Arlee, back to their usual chirpy self, but they didn't let go of Rina's hand, and she was glad for the comfort.

CHAPTER TWELVE

THE MARTLET on a Sunday evening wasn't as busy or as boisterous as it was on a Friday or a Saturday night, and that meant that Aerten's shift was pretty relaxed. Tegan, the landlady, had ushered her over when she'd arrived, and now she was sat in between the bar and the kitchen, sipping a lemonade and keeping an eye on all and sundry.

Tegan was at the bar, the plump, white-haired young woman pulling pints; over by the dartboard was a cluster of farmers, a handful of half-empty pint glasses scattered on the table behind them, and in their hands; and by the door were her Hunt, quaffing ale and getting through an alarming number of halloumi sticks.

She grinned. Usually, she'd have wandered over and chatted with them for a bit, stolen the odd halloumi stick, but this evening she didn't want anything to dim the glow she felt from those hours lying amongst the poppies with Rina.

At some point she'd have to revisit the nightmare that was Andraste, being in *here*, in her *new home* and... No. No. Focus on the glow.

One of the older teenagers from the village saw her smile,

and tried to sneak past her to the kitchen. She stuck her arm out to block his path without blinking. "No."

"No?"

He looked like he was about to say something else so she repeated the word, just once, and let her years of leading men in battle infuse her voice with warning. "No."

It happened every now and then, some foolish teenager with some kind of death wish. It wasn't so bad if she caught them, but if Tegan did… That had definitely been something to behold; she'd grabbed the youth by the ear, dragged him out the pub, and banned him for a month.

There was a quiet cough from behind her, and when she turned around, on the bar was a basket of chips and a jug of that deliciously thick gravy that Leah made so well, and the kitchen door was closing.

Aerten had only met Leah once, on her first day, when Tegan had brought her into the kitchen and introduced her to the quiet chef. A Welsh lilt coloured her voice and she could barely look up without flushing and wanting to hide. Aerten instinctively knew that this was someone who needed protection, and she'd been right because Tegan had looked at her and she'd just *known*.

Neither of them knew exactly what made Leah so skittish, but she seemed like a sweet girl, and they'd be damned if they were going to let her be bothered by anyone.

Unfortunately, the teenagers in the village had seemed to take it as some kind of challenge, hence Aerten's position by the kitchen door. And if Leah showed her thanks with cooked food, then who was she to argue?

She dipped a chip into the gravy and smiled as she took a bite. Perfect.

Tegan headed over to where she sat and stole a chip. "You look pleased with yourself."

Aerten couldn't help herself; she grinned the kind of self-satisfied grin that could only mean one thing.

"Oh yeah?" Tegan waggled her eyebrows. "Let me in on your secret; it's been far too long since I got any."

Laughing, Aerten grabbed another chip. "Like you couldn't change that any time you wanted." She gestured over to the Hunt's table, where Deuroc was gazing over at the landlady, a lovesick look in his eyes.

"Ah," Tegan straightened slightly. "But we both know that he's not a one and done kind of guy; if I gave an inch, he'd try and have me walking down an aisle, and that's just not me." Her eyes softened for a moment as she looked at Deuroc who was now very studiously reading the menu. "I'm a one and done kind of girl."

Aerten very much doubted that, but she wasn't about to argue with her boss. "That makes sense."

"Does it?" Tegan looked suspicious, but let it go, and dropped her own line of questioning. Aerten was pretty pleased with herself for getting out of that one.

She was about to ask the landlady for a top up of lemonade, when the door to the pub opened and she shivered.

"What the fuck do you think you're doing?" A very mild looking farmer, whom Aerten had never heard raise his voice much above a whisper, was red in the face and fronting off with one who looked like he was way beyond retirement age. Someone shoved someone else, and she realised that she was going to have to break up a scuffle, which seemed ridiculous.

Striding over, she grabbed each of them by the collar and dragged them apart. "No fighting in the pub gentlemen."

"Bitch," one of them spat, and Aerten felt some long locked away anger rise, and his face was overlayed with face after face of every man, every soldier, every leader who'd ever tried to defy her leadership. Men who'd challenged her, spat upon her and... She dropped them both and staggered backwards, covering her eyes so she didn't have to see, to relive the violence that had been visited upon her and Brianne over and over. Only closing her eyes didn't make any difference, because these memories were seared in to her brain, into her memory and–

She stopped. Opened her eyes. And looked straight at where Andraste, Goddess of War was standing before her.

"Out."

"Come now, don't you think that–"

Aerten didn't falter, didn't even pause for a moment, before she grabbed the goddess by the hair and dragged her out of the pub, throwing her to the ground.

Andraste leaned back, ignoring the gravel that must have been cutting into her hands, and laughed.

The sound inside the pub seemed to have quietened, which Aerten took to mean that removing the goddess had removed the source of the anger. Turning on her heel, she went to walk away, to try and remove herself from that oh-so-familiar rage that she didn't know how to quench without fighting, but a single word stopped her in her tracks. A name.

"Brianne."

CHAPTER THIRTEEN

INTERLUDE

THE WARRIOR PRINCESS paused and Andraste felt a sting of satisfaction. It was not fair that Aerten was here, alive, wearing her sister's face, when Brianne was, Brianne was...

She didn't want to believe it. Couldn't believe. But the anger Aerten had shown the previous day had been true enough, and it had not been so many centuries that she did not remember how bluntly truthful Aerten was. It had always been Brianne's favourite thing about her twin.

"She's fierce and a born leader," *Brianne had said,* "but she never knows when to keep her mouth shut. Says the truth even when it made it worse for us." *The priestess princess had smiled then, sad and sorrowful.* "I'd have taken far more to hear her defy and cut them down like that once more."

That hadn't been the whole truth though. In the weeks and months after the attack on the princesses, even after their mother had coerced three tribes of men to follow her lead, Brianne had awoken screaming almost every single night.

That's how Andraste had found her first. Boudicca had petitioned her many times over the years, and she'd somewhat paid attention, but it was the cries of her daughter that made Andraste burn for revenge.

And revenge they'd had.

They'd razed whole cities to the ground, and scorched the earth with men's screams, but still Brianne had sobbed in Andraste's arms each night after battle. Because that was where she'd found herself. Holding this woman with so much love and so much passion to give, but so terrified and shaking that Andraste only kissed her with a gentleness that she hadn't known herself capable of.

"You dare to mention her name to me?"

The warrior princess' words dragged Andraste to the present, and leaning back she revelled in the cut of sharp stones beneath her hands. Her scalp ached where her hair had been pulled, but still this physical pain was better, better than knowing...

"What happened?"

"What hap–are you toying with me? *You* happened. You supported us, made us fight and kill and burn in your name, and then, when we needed you most, you were nowhere to be seen. We loosed your hare, prepared ourselves for battle and not eighty thousand of us fell in exchange for four hundred of they. We who had taken whole cities before us, gone. Dead."

"You are yet alive." *The poisonous glare that Aerten sent her would have slain Andraste on the spot, were she not made of stronger mettle than that. But it was true. For all her protestations, she was still alive and her sister was not.*

"The Wild Hunt. They took Brianne and I, mounted us on horses and saved us from the wreckage of that massacre. And I wanted to live, burned to avenge my family, my people, those I'd led into battle to die but Brianne..." *Aerten's voice trailed away.* "Brianne mourned you. She cried out for you and she searched for you, and when she finally realised, as I had a century before, that you had truly abandoned us, she killed herself."

There were more words spoken, of that Andraste was sure, but she doubted she would ever be able to recount them. After, she recalled a ringing in her ears, and she must have fallen backward because she was on the floor, looking up at the sky. It was dark and star-filled, and yet the sight of it bought her no pleasure, not even after millennia trapped behind the Veil. She felt blank, empty, as if the colour in this world too was draining into some unknown Otherworld beyond her reach.

She wondered if Brianne was there, vivid red hair blowing in the breeze as she stood amongst the groves she'd so loved and laughed – laughed like Andraste had never seen, like she'd never been so broken by the greed and violence of men.

Something salty dropped upon her lips, and she blinked up at where Aerten's face loomed above her, out of focus and desperately, desperately sad. She was tasting Aerten's tears. Tears for the twin she'd lost, the faith in her goddess she'd abandoned, and the life she would never have.

And for the first time, Andraste tasted despair.

CHAPTER FOURTEEN

THE PUB WAS NEARLY silent by the time Aerten walked back in. The farmer who'd called her a bitch stumbled over, shamefaced and apologetic for something that wasn't his fault, and she nodded an acceptance of his apology. She ignored the men of the Hunt who surrounded her, asking their questions.

Was she okay? *No.*

They'd have continued asking if Tegan hadn't dismissed them from the bar with a wave of her hand. "We're closing," she announced to muttered disappointment, but the Martlet had seen more excitement in one hour than it had all year, and everyone wanted to leave and wipe the distaste for the night's events from their shoes.

Only Sten lingered, ever silent.

"I'm fine. Go ahead, I'll walk home." Her words were hoarse and she knew he didn't quite believe them, but he nodded anyway, and ushered Herla and Morcant and Deuroc out with him.

When the last had left, and Tegan had locked the door behind them, she pointed at a corner table. "Sit."

Aerten obeyed, glad to be told what to do for once.

"You can't do that. It's one thing ejecting someone from the pub for being drunk and disorderly, but dragging them out by their hair after they've done nothing wrong…" her voice trailed off as she saw the tracks tears were making down Aerten's cheeks.

"You're right. I apologise. It won't ever happen again, but she was not…she'd caused…" She didn't know how to explain to this landlady, this kind woman who'd given her a job and somehow become her friend, that all the trouble that had come on suddenly had been due to the influence of an ancient war goddess. That simply wasn't believable.

"Oh fuck," said Tegan, her voice suddenly very serious. "She was a 'special' kind of trouble, huh?" She said the word special as if it meant anything but, and Aerten was taken aback by the tiredness in her voice. "I fucking hate that kind of trouble. Next time, tell me."

Aerten was about to ask what on earth some mortal in a pub could do, but there was a weariness in Tegan's eyes that made her stop and reassess. "I will."

Someone cleared their throat and both women looked up to see Leah standing by the table, long dark hair hiding her face. "You should see someone."

"See someone?" Aerten didn't know what she meant.

"A therapist, because your trauma–" Leah's cut off suddenly, as if she were struggling to speak. There was a pause and then she continued, as if forcing the words out of her mouth. "You have to deal with your trauma, or it will control you. Therapists help. They talk. Give you coping strategies. You're less alone."

She blinked back the tears that threatened to spill once more and nodded her thanks gruffly. "I will. Thank you, Leah."

"You're welcome. Tegan, I will clean up and exit out the

back," and then Leah was retreating, practically running, back to the safety of the kitchen.

"Wow," said Tegan. "Leah must like you. I've never heard her say as many words as that in one go before."

Aerten wiped her eyes with the back of her hand and tried a tremulous smile. "She's a sweet girl."

"I'm not a girl," an indignant voice came from the kitchen. "I'm twenty-five!"

They looked at each other, laughed, and mouthed 'girl'.

Aerten walked home, and when she got in, she was touched to see that the rest of the Hunt was waiting up for her; even Morcant who usually stayed at Kenna's. They didn't say much, didn't need to, but sat with her in comfortable silence by the fire. Even the Hound left Sten to sit across her feet, and shuffled around each time she felt a little like crying.

In all her years as part of the Wild Hunt, the men had never been much for talking. They'd argued, sure but those arguments had never really been resolved as such. They merely fumed at each other in relative silence until one or both of them got over it, and then things were back to normal again. But they didn't talk about their pain; about the pain of having seen their people – their way of life – die and fade out of existence.

"Ahem." Herla cleared his throat. "Do you want to, you know, talk?" He looked exceedingly uncomfortable and the warmth of affection that she felt for him took Aerten by surprise.

"It's okay."

The relief across his face was apparent, even if he attempted to hide it. "Are you sure?"

She smiled. "I'm sure."

"There's beer," piped up Deuroc, and then "What?!" when the others turned on him with glares.

Sten leaned over to where the Hound sat across her feet, and ruffled his ears. "Talking is good."

They all looked at him. Sten was not exactly known for his verbosity. Aerten felt a gurgle of laughter rising and they all looked more than a little alarmed when she let it free.

"It's the shock," said Morcant.

"The shock?" If Aerten could have paused her laughter, she'd have been able to explain the concept to Herla, but she couldn't. She just kept laughing as they began to bicker around her. They might not have been her original family, but they acted like one, and that was all that mattered to her.

IT WAS dark when Rina woke up, just a chink of sunlight breaking through the curtains. Arlee was curled up against her side, mouth wide open, adorable little snuffles emanating from their mouth, and Kenna appeared to have crawled in her sleep as far away from the both of them on the sofa that she could get. They were both completely out for the count.

She eased herself out from under the blankets and crept out towards the kitchen without waking them.

Arlee's kitchen opened out onto their back garden, which wasn't really a back garden as much as it was the edge of the forest. There was some grass, some chairs that Rina didn't think Arlee had ever covered with the tarpaulin that lay on the ground next to them, and a small metal table that Kenna had forged as a housewarming gift.

After turning on the kettle and brewing some – she shuddered – instant coffee, she opened the back door and stepped out, barefoot, onto the grass.

It was never this peaceful when Arlee was awake, which Rina never minded because Arlee had this uncanny way of knowing whatever it was you needed, without you ever telling them, but right now it seemed like the perfect space.

The kettle boiled and she poured her coffee. Milk. A little sugar. Simple quiet steps of a routine that allowed her brain to focus on the actual things it needed to think about. Like last night.

She sat on one of the garden chairs, blew and sipped her coffee. Was she really that closed off? The insights last night, about her not knowing how to deal with vulnerability, scared her. Rina knew that relationships meant allowing some vulnerability around the other person, at least, and she'd done that. She'd cried in Aerten's arms, talked to her in the poppy fields, and still ended up emotionally drained from it all.

Another sip.

Perhaps it was something you could learn? A capacity for vulnerability seemed like a good life skill to have, and she liked to think that she was very good at practicalities, so surely she could just teach herself this. And yet…

Another sip.

She heard birds singing in the trees and she closed her eyes and leaned back. Perhaps it was not so much about making herself super vulnerable all of the time, but rather just not shutting everyone out. Allowing them to see past the wall and professional, organised Rina that she showed the world.

Okay. This would take time, and it would take practice. Maybe she could practice with Aerten?

It hit her then, an unexpected vision that stole her breath and had her hurtling through an ever-turning carousel of colour. It was dizzying and she thought she might actually throw up when the carousel came to a sudden stop and she was looking at the clearest picture that magic had ever shown her. Andraste was walking through a grove of trees where bodies of men hung, mutilated and bloody. And in the middle of the grove stood three women: one elder, and two who were clearly sisters, twins probably Rina thought. And one of them was Aerten. All three women were covered in woad and blood and the fierceness in their eyes almost made Rina stumble back, away. But when the carousel slowly began to start up again, she threw herself back out into the grove.

The women didn't see her, but Andraste did, eyes flashing as she approached. *"Who dares enter my sacred grove?"*

Rina was shaking, the goddess' power magnified a thousand times from what she'd felt in the library. "Rina. Rina Baroni. Andraste, you know me. We met."

The goddess' face remained as stone. *"You lie."*

"No, no! I promise. This is a vision, I'm an oracle. You must remember."

"The value in visions is that they don't know how powerful they are until after. Fine then, Oracle. Watch and prepare, because the day will come when I will call upon you." She turned her back and stalked over to where Boudicca, for it could only be Boudicca, stood with her daughters. *"The time for battle commences once more. You have done me proud."*

"Thank you." The twin who wasn't Aerten spoke up. "You honour us, gracious goddess."

The warmth with which Andraste gazed upon that downturned head made Rina gasp, and the goddess frowned, the moment clearly broken. *"One last fight, and you shall fly on the wings of victory, avenged and revenged. Go. Prepare for battle."*

As they walked past her, unseeing, Rina almost reached out to touch this strange, unsmiling Aerten, with woad upon her face.

"She cannot hear or see you," said the goddess from behind her. *"That is the curse of the Oracle, to ever see those departed, and to be ever just out of reach."*

"That seems cruel."

"Such is the way of our world."

In the distance, Rina heard the sound of drums. "Why did you abandon them?"

The goddess turned on her, full fury hitting Rina so hard she fell to the ground. *"Abandon them? I would never abandon them Oracle, lest I was myself taken from this place."* She looked around the grove and smiled. It was not a pleasant smile. *"These sacrifices, they keep me strong against the gods who'd take my lands, take my victories as their own!"*

But even as she spoke, she seemed unsure, looking past Rina as if to another figure, standing behind her. Rina looked, but there was no one there.

"You dare come here Victoria? A Roman goddess amongst my people? In my grove?" But as she spoke, she faded a little, as if someone were attempting to erase her from a larger picture, and when Rina looked behind her this time, a female figure started coming into view. As if she'd been hidden behind a curtain, and now the curtain was being drawn back.

"Oracle," Andraste's voice was faint now, *"I will come back. I will return to my people. To my Bri–"* And she was gone.

Rina was still sitting outside when Arlee and Kenna came to find her.

Once Andraste had faded away, she'd been thrown back out the vision, through the kaleidoscope of doom, until she came to in Arlee's garden. And she sat there, not really moving, clutching at a mug of coffee that had long gone cold.

Her friends exchanged looks.

"Rina," wheedled Arlee, "do you want to come inside hun?"

"No, thank you."

"Are you sure?"

"Quite sure, thank you."

"For fuck's sake." Kenna slapped her palm down on the

table and they all jumped. "We literally talked about this last night Rina; fucking *talk to us.*"

"And what would you like me to tell you? That my girlfriend used to be a warrior and kill people and string them up in trees? That I just saw her walk to the battle that would massacre her entire people, and I couldn't stop it? That some fucking goddess," she slammed the mug down on the table and it shattered. She stopped. Sighed. "Come out then – not you two," she said to Kenna and Arlee who were clearly about to say something along the lines of 'we *are* out'. "Andraste."

For the first time since she'd seen her, the warrior goddess' face was bare. *"You were that Oracle."*

"Yes." She felt a surge of anger rise like bile in her throat, and she caught it quickly and glared at Andraste. "Stop that. Or at least, turn it the fuck down. Please. I'm too tired for anger."

The goddess inclined her head.

Kenna stared. "You don't feel like Belisama."

Andraste gave a derisory snort. *"Like a light goddess? I should think not. She's fuelled by the earth and the seasons; I'm fuelled by you mortals – far more chaotic and capricious."* She circled Kenna for a moment. *"Though I haven't had a priestess like you in quite some time. How would you like some victory in your life, dragon shifter?"*

There was a huff and Andraste jumped back before the flames emanating from Kenna's mouth could singe her. *"My my, as touchy as your goddess too. Never mind, I'm after something different anyway."* She looked at Rina. *"I don't need a priestess. I need an Oracle. And you are going to come with me. Now."*

And before Rina could say another word, there was a tug and the world moved sideways.

CHAPTER FIFTEEN

AERTEN AWOKE to a furious tiny Arlee pummelling her awake.

"What the–?"

"She's *gone*!" wailed Arlee, "she's gone and you're the only one who can find her because you're the only one who knows this psycho of a goddess."

She looked over at where the rest of the Hunt were standing in her doorway with Kenna, worry etched across their faces and sleep fell away from her instantly.

Sitting up in bed, she leaned over to grab a top from her dresser, barely cognisant of the Hunt and Kenna averting their eyes and backing awkwardly away from her nakedness. Arlee did neither. "What happened?"

They sat down heavily on the edge of the bed and spoke so fast Aerten had to focus to understand. "She had another vision and then we were talking to her and then Andraste was there and then they were talking and then they were both gone."

"Gone? Gone where?"

"How the fuck am I supposed to know?" spat out Arlee. "I

don't have magical powers; I can't turn into a dragon or have visions or live for two thousand years. *Why the hell don't one of you who can, do something?!*"

Aerten closed her eyes and tried to slow down her rapidly increasing pulse. She needed to get to that quiet place that she used to retreat to before a battle, that place inside of her that was so focused that everything else faded away. She'd not done that in centuries, preferring to leave the violence of her past behind her, but desperate times…

Everything slowed.

Arlee's mouth was moving but slower that Aerten had ever seen; the Hunt's awkward shuffling became a slow two-step; even the ticks of the timepiece on her bedside table slowed down until there were whole minutes between each sound.

Aerten had no magic of her own, not really, but she did have the ability to focus harder than anyone she'd ever met. She'd never known whether it was the world slowing down or her mind speeding up, but it was like shrugging on an old cloak that she'd cast off. It fit her. Comfortably. And with it a flash of the past that quickly faded away until Aerten could breathe, safe in the knowledge that she was no longer the warrior princess on the warpath. She would not turn back into the angry, bitter woman who'd burnt cities to the ground alongside her mother and sister.

But she would find Rina. Of that she was certain.

IT WAS quiet atop Firle Beacon.

Rina heard the birds circling above, the wind whispering through the grass and for a moment everything else melted away.

The last time she'd been here, she'd been desperately digging up her brother, and it had been night, the hill blanketed in darkness. But now it was morning and the sun's rays shone across the Downs, kissing the tops of trees and hedgerows that crisscrossed fields. It was peaceful, and she felt her body sigh out, releasing some of the tension it held.

Andraste stood beside her. *"It's beautiful."*

"Yes." Rina couldn't even find it in herself to be angry with the goddess. "Yes it is."

"The Veil was..." her voice cut out suddenly, as if she were struggling to compose herself. *"It was grey. Washed out, as if everything had been painted in black and white. We didn't see this. We barely saw anything, trapped out of our lands, our home, away from..."* Her voice stopped again.

"From Brianne?" Rina wasn't sure what prompted her to ask, but the anguish in the goddess' eyes answered her question better than any words could. "I saw what happened, with Victoria in the grove."

"I know that now. You were the Oracle I saw that day. Somehow, it wasn't until you'd actually had the vision, that I could see your face clearly." Andraste turned towards Rina and Rina fought the urge to step backward. *"But you still don't want to be my Oracle."*

Pausing, Rina said slowly, "Say I did help you with a vision, just the once mind, what would you want to see?"

"Not what, who."

"There'd be conditions."

The goddess laughed bitterly, *"I would expect nothing less. What would you ask of me?"*

"For you to agree for a one-time-only vision."

"With the right to ask for others?"

Rina nodded. "The right to ask, but you'd have to take my answer each time as final. No kidnapping my brother, no threats, and no hurting the people I care about – either to get me to have a vision, or for any other reason."

"Acceptable. Is that all?" Andraste seemed pleasantly surprised.

"No. You need to talk to Aerten. You need to explain what happened without whipping her up into a frenzy. She needs to understand that you didn't just abandon her and her family and her people to die."

The acquiescence was slower this time. *"She might not want to talk to me."*

"I know. She may not be ready to talk to you for years, but when she is, you will drop everything and come."

The look Andraste shot her was one of bitter bemusement. *"You feel for her as I did for her sister."*

Rina felt herself flush. "That is neither here not there. Do we have an agreement?"

"Yes, Oracle, we have an agreement." The goddess' words were imbued with power that the librarian hadn't been expecting, almost as if in speaking the words, she'd written them upon Rina's skin. A branded promise between them both. It made her shiver, and she wondered whether she was doing the right thing.

"What do you wish to see?"

Andraste held out her hand to Rina, laughing softly when she hesitated to take it. *"Come Oracle, you did promise."*

"Yes, but I usually…"

"I am Goddess. I can help direct your visions, use you as a conduit. It will different from before."

Rina took her hand.

It was instant; no carousel ride through multicolours, or a headrush that pushed her along. She was simply back in the grove again.

Andraste let go of her hand and walked to where her past self was stood with Brianne, and before Rina could say anything, she kind of just floated into the other body, until there was just one Andraste. The Andraste holding Brianne in her arms.

This was her farewell to her lover, Rina realised. Andraste could not change what had happened, could not change the course of history because if she'd done that, it would already have happened. But she could have one last night in her sacred grove, and love the woman that she'd lost without even knowing.

Rina stepped outside the grove and sat on the floor, back against one of the trees, and let Andraste have her moment.

CHAPTER SIXTEEN

BY NOON, Aerten was ready to storm the Veil itself. All the focusing and searching had led to nothing, and she had almost resorted to begging Kenna to ask Belisama for help.

"Yeah, I'm not sure that's a great idea. My goddess has her own way of interpreting requests for aid, and I'm not necessarily sure it'd give you a result you actually want."

Sten's hand on Aerten's shoulder was the only reason she didn't slam her hands down on the kitchen table in frustration.

"Outside." She had to bite her tongue to stop her from cursing at him. She was really in no mood to have someone tell her how she should be responding. Rina was gone. They'd searched the village, driven around, and nothing. Arlee had been right; what good was all the history, power, if it meant that one of their own could snatched away at any moment.

"Aerten. Outside." She pushed up off the chair and stomped out the back door, hearing it snick shut as Sten followed her.

"You fucking dare-" A staff fell at her feet. "What is this?"

"A staff."

"I can see that Sten. Why have you thrown me one?"

He didn't answer, merely gathering up his long silver hair into a bun atop his head, and then taking up a stance, with another staff in his hands.

He wanted to fight her?

If it had been anyone else, Aerten would have seen it as a challenge, but from Sten…? She looked at him and he looked straight back at her, his eyes calm and measured. Oh. He wanted to help her channel her frustration. She leaned down and picked up the staff, weighing it in her hands until she got the balance of it. "No axes?"

His gruff laugh startled her. "You'd best me for sure with an axe. But a staff…?"

"Oh I can best you with a staff also," and she swung it once through the air, breathing with the curve of its fall, feeling herself settle into the familiarity. Muscle memory from centuries past. As he brought his up to meet hers, the crack of wood on wood made her sigh and then she lost herself to the motions. The parries and thrusts came as easily to her as they had when she was first mortal, a comfort that she was able to let go and settle into.

They must have been fighting for about half an hour when she felt a gust of breath across her neck as someone walked up behind her. Without flinching, Aerten spun round and shoved them backwards, her staff coming to rest upon their forehead.

"You!" Her fury was unabaited at the sight of Andraste, even as Rina came up between them, and put her arm on Aerten's. "You took Rina from me. Took someone else. *Again.*"

"Stop."

She turned to look at her librarian, dark hair mussed all over the place, as if she'd been caught in a strong wind.

"Stop? *Stop?!* She took you, Rina. Like you she took your brother. Just turning people's lives upside down once more without even a shadow of regret. What she has done, what she did to my people, *to my sister*, can never be undone."

Rina's eyes flashed and Aerten was taken aback by the fierceness in her face. "Do not speak to me like that."

Aerten realised that her hands were shaking, the staff resting on Andraste's forehead trembling, and she let go. Dropping the stick and stepping backwards. "You don't know." Her voice was hoarse and suddenly her whole body was shaking, her legs gave way and she dropped to her knees on the grass.

Rina was right there next to her, cupping Aerten's face with palms that cooled her feverish skin. "Tell me?"

She cried then. Cried for the girl that she'd once been, joyful and innocent and happy. Cried for her father, whose legacy had been decimated by a Roman emperor who did not keep his vows. Cried for her sister and her mother and herself, for the indignations and violations that they'd suffered. She cried for her people that she'd led, and for the people that she'd killed, and she cried because she knew she would never be the same.

"I didn't abandon you." The words were quiet and pained, and when she looked up, she saw Andraste's faced streaked with tears of woad. *"I would never have abandoned you. You, or your mother, or Brianne. I saw what they did, and they all deserved to burn for it. But I, like you, got dragged behind the Veil and could not escape, no matter how hard I tried."*

"You lie."

"Aerten, darling, I saw it." Rina was there, holding her, and in her eyes she saw truth.

She tried to get control of herself, deep shuddery sobs slowing as she focused, processing this new information. "You didn't abandon us."

"*No.*"

She pushed upwards, grabbing staff for balance, and shook her head as Rina stepped close. "When did you-"

"This morning, just before she, well." Before Andraste had taken her.

"You're going to stop doing that." Her words to the goddess weren't a question, and Andraste inclined her head slowly. "I…I need… I need time. Please."

Sten and Andraste left, but as Rina went to go back inside, Aerten caught her hand. "Serch, I don't want to lose you."

"You won't," Rina's eyes were dark, searching, as if looking for a truth of her own. "I'm not going anywhere."

"I don't want to feel that pain anymore." Once, Aerten would have thought such an admission a sign of weakness, but now she knew it for what it was; the strength to ask for help. "You said something about, what was it, a therapist?"

Rina smiled, "That's a good idea; we can find you a therapist." She leaned forward and gently pressed her lips to Aerten's. "You've got this. And you've got me." She didn't say 'I love you', but she didn't need to. They both heard it anyway.

"And you have me, serch, you have me."

EPILOGUE

TEGAN WAS LESS than impressed when she closed up that evening, to find Latis sat at the bar when she walked back inside. Fuck.

"What do you want?"

The Goddess of Water and Beer raised an empty pint glass. *"A beer?"*

Sighing, the landlady made her way round behind the bar to pull a pint. "I haven't seen you for a couple of years. It's been nice without you causing trouble."

"There are many taverns that earn my patronage." The goddess grinned, tossing her blonde hair over one shoulder and lifting the full pint up to her lips. *"So many pints being pulled, so much havoc in the aftermath."*

"And yet you find your way back here."

"It's interesting here."

It was not interesting in Tunford. That was precisely why Tegan's family had lived there for generations. It was quiet and it was boring, and most of all, it was not interesting. Or at least, it had been until the newcomers strode into town and brought with them such a stink of magic that Tegan had to fight not to let on that she could sense it.

"Besides, it has not been 'a couple' of years Tegan, it has been seven."

Seven years.

Seven blissfully peaceful years. Which could only mean … Tegan cursed. This was not good. How could that much time have passed without her realising it?

Latis drained her glass, and placed it on the bar, and when she meet Tegan's eyes, her eyes were pools of water, with unfathomable depths. *"Yes Tegan, that means that it's time for the Ghost Dog to return. And I intend to be here to watch the ensuing chaos."*

Married in Moonlight

A GODSTOUCHED SAPPHIC ROMANCE

ALI WILLIAMS

DIANA TRIFORMIS

It had been many years since she had walked these hills, taking in the sights and the sounds of the South Downs. It made her nostalgic for years gone by, for years spent with people who worshipped them. Each part of her struggled for dominance, wanting to feel the sensations of the living, of this magic that flowed like a fountain, granting new life and shredding the Veil as if it were merely made from thread.

Shaking her head, once, twice, thrice, she split into the three aspects of herself, each part walking separately, but with their voices and heads echoing in each other's minds as if they were still one.

Diana, the Huntress, led the way. Tall, imposing, never afraid to take the lead. Her hair flowed around her like a cloak, and the horns atop her head were reminiscent of a stag's. She liked that she got to keep those.

"You always were a show off," muttered Hecate, even as her own hands twitched, longing to open a portal, setting a crossroads in this realm, in this place. Hecate was dressed in black, surprise surprise, and had her hair cropped so short, it looked as if it had been painted onto her scalp.

Luna of the Moon said nothing. Just followed the other two, bathing in the moonbeams that cast light across the Downs, smiling with as each step drew power to her. She almost glowed with the strength of it, and when she sighed, her relief flooded the other two so much that they paused to look at her.

"Luna?"

"Yes?" Her voice breathed through them.

"You okay there?" Hecate's words were both amused and a little biting. The look Luna turned on her made her draw back. "I was just asking."

"It's unnecessary when you feel as I do," replied the moon goddess.

"Enough," said Diana, striding forward with decisive movements. "We have not the time for such squabbles. We know where we are headed. Let us go there." A slow smile spread across her face and there was not an ounce of kindness in it. "Andraste's reckoning awaits her."

RINA

Rina closed the door behind her and leaned against it with a sigh.

Getting married was stressful.

She loved her family, but there were *so fucking many of them*. Everywhere she turned there were more Baronis, all loud and excited and ready for her to get married – even if it was in the middle of the night, and not in a Catholic church.

That hadn't been the conversation that she thought it'd have been, but then again, when you were marrying another woman, that wasn't really an option.

Her mum and aunt had argued that God with a capital G would be watching over and blessing their union, no matter where it was anyway. What they hadn't realised, was that the person presiding over the ceremony was a literal goddess. Andraste the Indestructible. Rina wasn't entirely certain that having a war deity officiate her marriage was the best decision in the world, but somehow Andraste and Aerten had become close and she'd definitely rather have Andraste on her side than anyone else's.

"Rina."

Speak of the goddess.

"Why are you hiding in this tiny room?"

Rina looked around at the cleaning supplies in the closet that she'd hidden in, and then back at the ancient goddess, "Because my family are out there. And they all want to poke and prod at me some more."

Andraste considered this answer. *"Where would you like to be instead?"*

There were many places that Rina would like to be, the main being *not* in the cleaning supplies closet of a barn, hiding from her over-enthusiastic family. In fact, the one place she wanted to be above all else, was with Aerten, and that simply wasn't possible right now.

"Nonsense," said Andraste briskly, and Rina shivered, as she always did when the goddess took a peek inside her mind. *"I don't see why you can't go to Andraste. You are marrying her after all."*

And before Rina could protest, she nodded, and then they slipped sideways until they were in Aerten's room and her fiancée was blinking in surprise at the unexpected visitors.

Squawking, she ran and hid behind the wall of men that had moved to stand in front of Aerten. As much as they had accepted the fact that Andraste was sticking around, the Freed Hunt – formerly of the Wild Hunt – were not very trusting of ancient deities. Rina couldn't blame them, what with having being trapped in the Hinterlands for centuries, by one such deity.

"Serch? Are you…? Why are you hiding from me?"

"It's bad luck for you to see me, the day of the wedding!"

The other woman's voice was low and comforting though, and Rina wanted nothing more than to throw herself in her fiancée's arms and let all her stresses float away.

There was a pause and then Sten, one of Aerten's groomsmen, and previous member of the Wild Hunt suggested, "Well, if you're getting married at midnight, then surely it's not technically the same day."

That tooka good few minutes for Rina to consider and process, before she pushed the Hunt out of the way and threw herself at her fiancée.

Aerten was wearing a suit; it was fitted with sleeves that nataurally showed off her forearms and to be perfectly truthful, that short-circuited Rina's brain for a moment, and then she was telling the men to get out, asking Andraste to leave (politely, because war goddess), and reaching up to pull Aerten's lips atop hers and kissing her as if her life depended on it.

Hands entangled in her hair, messing up the beautiful styling that her aunt had spent over an hour on, but she didn't care. All she cared about was Aerten, Aerten, Aerten, touching her, holding her, and kissing her so sweetly she thought she might swoon.

Coming up for breath, Aerten leaned her forehead against Rina's and Rina found her pulse slowing down, relaxing, and everything suddenly felt alright again.

"Serch, what happened?"

"They just kept trying to make me look all perfect and it feels so weird."

There was a huff of laughter,. "But you always look perfect."

"Exactly! I don't need makeup and daisies in my hair and…" Rina's voice trailed off as she saw Aerten clock the flowers, and then look back at her with a warmth that she felt all the way down in her toes. "Okay, the flowers can stay, but no more foundation! It feels like my skin is suffocating!"

"well, we can't have that," murmured her fiancée, and then she was being kissed again. Thoroughly. It was really rather thrilling.

They were beginning to lose sight of why they were there

– midnight wedding ceremony ditched in favour of making out – when there was a sharp knock on the door and Kenna's voice said, "Not to disrupt whatever shenanigans are happening in there, but if I don't take you back to your room Rina, I think your mother might have a literal breakdown."

The two women broke apart and sighed.

"I'm coming!" Rina called.

"It will be okay," reassured Aerten. "I promise."

"Of course it will be," replied Rina. "Tonight I get to be officially yours forever." And the she took one last look at her bride to be, drinking in every inch of her face, and then ran out into the hallway.

ANDRASTE

Something was not right.

Andraste was out on the Downs, looking out over the chairs that had been arranged for the ceremony. The ribbons for the handfasting were tied to her belt, and she'd be able to draw them, no problem. Belisama had been cajoled by Kenna into attending and lighting the event. Lanterns and candles were arranged beautifully, so that the field the ceremony was taking place in was perfectly lit. Andraste wasn't even certain the sun would have been able to do a better job. Chairs were all in place, people were milling about quite happily. Everything seemed *to be fine.*

And yet she knew that something was just not right.

There was an echo on the wind, and Andraste listened, not entirely sure what she was expecting to hear; perhaps warriors from a bygone age, shadows on the wind, accompanying Aerten, their warrior princess, into life's most defining battle.

Andraste hid a smile. Rina had told her in no uncertain terms that she was not to refer to marriage as a battle.

"There's too much power in your words," *she'd pointed out.* "I'm not risking it."

Power, she thought suddenly. That's what it feels like.

It didn't feel like power that was natural to the land though, and it wasn't just one strand. One... Two... Three... And words on the wind that had brought them to her notice. "Andraste... we're coming for you."

One of the candles snuffed out, and Andraste shot a look at Belisama; had that been intentional? The nod that the other goddess gave her confirmed it. She felt it too.

"You." *She gestured to the bridesperson who'd been assigned to keep an eye on them. The Arlee person was so diminutive that most people overlooked them, but Andraste had been on the receiving end of a lecture from them more than once. She saw why Rina had asked them to keep the goddesses company.*

Arlee merely raised an eyebrow and refused to move.

"By the Earth you're a stubborn one. Fine. Arlee."

Arlee beamed and practically danced over, resplendent in a dark purple outfit that mirrored the other bridesmaid dresses, but split into two separate legs instead of a skirt. Andraste approved. It seemed very practical.

"There is something not quite right here. Belisama and I shall investigate. You need to get the mortals to go inside. I will not have this disrupting my oracle's day."

"You know how Rina feels about you saying my oracle." *Were they trying to be difficult? Now was not the time for semantics.*

"There is urgency. Do as I say." *She put a little bit more power into her words and Arlee stepped back before they caught themselves, and then glared.*

"You really are an arse," *they said, but still they moved towards the other guests, ushering them inside and talking about the possibility of rain.*

Belisama glided across the grass to stand by Andraste. "Well well, what is it that you've brought down upon us, Andraste?"

She didn't reply, instead searching the horizon for figures encroaching on their space, and sure enough, there were three figures, walking across the fields.

She would meet them, and she would put them in their places.

Only when she walked over, the three women who looked at her in surprise held none of the power that she'd felt on the wind. Instead they had that frisson of something surrounding them, the same something that had brought Rina to her attention.

More of the Godstouched. Were there not enough of them already running around this little village? Fate was playing a cruel trick on her.

"Who are you?" she demanded, not lessening the power in her tone. The women bristled, and all began talking at once. It was a veritable cacophony of voices.

"Well, I like that…"

"Rude!"

"The fucking audacity of some people."

"I mean, who the fuck are *you*?"

"Right? We don't recognise you."

"…and the bride is *our* cousin…"

Andraste shuddered and tried to block out some of the noise – to no avail. But she did recognise elements of her oracle in them. These must be of Rina's blood, which would explain why they felt Godstouched, and why they were more than a little stubborn.

"I am officiating the ceremony," she said. "You should go inside. It is likely to rain."

The one with what looked like war paint decorating her arms, looked up at the clear, star-studded sky and then back at her. "Want to try that again?"

She was struggling to come up with a suitable answer, when three voices in unison at her neck sent shivers down her spine.

"Andraste the Indestructible. Andraste the Terrible. Andraste the Doomed."

The three goddesses who stood behind her were clearly a triple goddess split in three. Each face almost shimmered when you looked at it, as if it were a mask and the other faces blurred beneath it. It was more than a little disconcerting for Andraste, who never interacted with a triple deity if she could help it, let alone the three mortal cousins of Rina that she was standing with.

"That is all a little dramatic," she said, reaching for the blood-drenched feel of her warrior power, that she'd buried deep down since she'd been back from behind the Veil. "What is it that I could possibly have done to you?"

"My hunters became the hunted," said one, and as each spoke, she knew them as if she had always known them. That was Diana, Italic goddess turned Roman.

"My moon shone upon their spilled blood," said Luna. Fuck Moon goddesses were known for being fairly protective of those who had their blessing. This wasn't shaping up well.

"And my crossroads showed them the way to the Underworld," said the final goddess, Hecate's words harsh on the air.

"What the...?" The redheaded cousin stared at Luna as if awestruck. "You're glowing."

Luna turned her head and there was a moment that Andraste recognised. When deities met the Godstouched that they were meant to meet, their *Godstouched mortal, there was a resonance in the air that they could feel in every shadow of their physical form. She felt it now, when Luna and this woman's eyes touched. And then another resonance, and then another, as the cousins locked eyes with the Goddesses, and their fates fell into place.*

Her oracle was not going to be happy about this.

RINA

Rina had just about gotten all of her family calmed down, when Arlee burst into the room, slightly wide-eyed and blurted out, "It's going to rain!"

Her mother and Aunt Vincenza ran out of the room immediately, her sister Bianca hot on their heels, dress gathered up in one hand, and swearing profusely as she went to check whether the buffet they'd laid outside was going to be okay.

Rina, however, did not panic. "Arlee?"

"Rina."

"Rain?"

Her friend paused, and looked apologetic. "Something's going on with Andraste; made me send everyone indoors. I couldn't..." They paused and pulled a face. "There was some kind of compulsion thing and I..." Their voice trailed off. "Your goddess is a fuckweasel, Rina."

Rina wanted to point out that Andraste was most certainly not *her* goddess, but she got the point. Arlee looked genuinely shaken, and Kenna went and pulled them into a hug.

"Goddesses be like that," their friend said. "Belisama likes me, and you know what she's like."

"Where is she now?" interjected Rina, because if she was going to have to do damage control on her fucking wedding day...

Arlee pointed outside and they moved to the window as one.

The moon was particularly bright, its beams highlighting a group in the distance that was comprised of Andraste, Rina's three cousins, and three women that she didn't recognise. She may not have recognised them, but her magic did, and she felt shivers rush through her.

Instantly, the three strange women and Andraste turned and stared right at her. That was not a pleasant feeling and instantly she knew. She *knew*.

She saw their pain and their hurt and the weight of the trauma that they'd carried so many years. It swept through her like a tsunami, crashing over every other emotion she felt until that was left was anger and grief.

So much grief.

It felt like Andraste's did, when the war goddess thought of Brianne. Aerten's sister had been the love of Andraste's life; there was nothing whimsical or fleeting about the intensity with which they had loved each other, and when Andraste had been pulled behind the Veil, separating her from Brianne, the perceived abandonment had resulted in Brianne's suicide.

Rina felt tears roll down her cheeks as all the grief that Diana, Luna, and Hecate – for those were their names, though she could not have told you how she knew – felt for those that they had lost, swamped her. It took her breath away and she began gasping for air.

It was too much, too intense, too much for her to bear.

And then she realised, those hundreds of lives they were grieving for? They'd been carrying that for centuries.

"Enough." Her voice was cold and detached, and sounded nothing like the ordinary librarian that she pretended she was. "I've had enough of this." She sent out a curse then, against fate and the universe, for allowing her to feel this pain, to be so Godstouched that their trauma could burden her from over a field away. But this curse, the words a throwaway moment, began so entangled in her power, that when she spoke, it was the Oracle speaking. "Enough pain, enough sadness. You do not have to feel this any longer. *I* do not have to feel this any longer."

Then she wobbled, and would have fallen to the floor if Aerten had not been there to catch her.

"Oh Serch," her fiancée said, cradling her in her arms. "You feel so deeply."

It was as if all of her power had fled her and for a moment, Rina wondered if she'd managed to rid herself of this cursed gift, but then she reached out and no, it was still there.

What was *not* still there, was the feeling of grief coming from the three goddesses with her cousins and Andraste. Pulling herself to her feet, she stumbled across to the window, where seven faces looked up at her in shock.

She could feel their magic still, flickers of individual pull of moon and forest and darkness. But that indefinable thing that she felt whenever she felt in the presence of an immortal, that souped up, charged to the high heavens power that seemed to accompany them? Gone.

Fuck. She'd turned Diana Triformis mortal.

AERTEN

Aerten stood by Andraste, under a bower of camellias that Rina's cousin Silvana had cultivated for their wedding. It looked so beautiful in the moonlight, the soft pink of the flowers almost luminescent. And when she lifted her head, she saw her Rina walking towards her.

In that moment, she didn't care about goddesses turned mortal, or any of the little squabbles that illustrated the day; all she cared about was getting to say 'I do' to her beautiful fiancée.

Life hadn't been easy. She'd literally watched everyone she'd ever loved die in front of her. And yet here she was, standing up with these men who had become her family, ready to marry the love of her life.

She glanced at where Rina's family sat, and they beamed at her. They'd made her feel like she was one of their own, and she loved them for it. And this small gathering – of the Hunt, of Rina's family and friends, Tegan and Leah – it felt right. Even if there were three ex-immortals sat in the back row, being watched over by a fairly bemused Belisama.

And then there was Rina.

Aerten had spent their courtship half waiting for the other shoe to drop, for something to happen to make Rina wake up and realise that a traumatised 2000 year old with trust issues was going to be far more work than she ever could have imagined.

But Rina never woke up, and neither did Aerten, and that was how she knew that none of this was a dream. It was real. As real as the shy smile Rina gave her when they clasped hands. As real as the ribbons that Andraste tied about their hands. And as real as their first kiss as wives.

"I love you," she whispered over and over, startled to find that her eyes had filled with tears. "My darling, my serch. I will always love you."

"I know," replied her wife. And Rina kissed her so softly Aerten could have almost dreamt the touch of those lips.

And in that moment, three things happened. First, the camellias began to bloom; the scent rising and the petals trembling until it seemed as if the bower itself were alive. Then the light of the moon surrounded them both until even the flames of the candles paled next to its brightness. And finally, when she looked to where the three strange goddesses were stood, right at the back, she saw Hecate do something with her hands.

Aerten gasped. Hecate, Goddess of the Crossroads was standing next to the ghost of her mother and her sister. They smiled at her, though Aerten could see that Brianne was crying. Turning round, when she saw Andraste's confusion, she realised that no one else could see them. Clasping hands with Rina, she willed a connection, anything, with her wife's magic so that she could see them too.

It took a moment, and perhaps a slight nudge from Hecate's own power, but when she heard Rina's slight inbreath, she knew that Rina could see them too.

"Oh," her wife breathed.

Her mother touched her hand to her heart, the great Boudicca showing her love for her only living daughter, and then shimmered out of existence. Brianne however, passed through the crowds of people until she stood face to face with Aerten. Reaching out, she went to touch Rina and smiled ruefully when her hand passed through. She walked through the men of the Hunt, as if granting each of them a little more strength, a thank you for keeping her sister company, and then she was next to Andraste, looking at the goddess with such love and such sorrow that in her moment of greatest happiness, Aerten thought her heart might break.

Then she leaned forward, kissed Andraste on the forehead, and vanished.

Looking across to where Hecate stood with Luna and Diana, Aerten mouthed *thank you* before her and Rina were swept up in a storm of familial well wishes.

But throughout it all, Rina never let go of her hand, and later, when they could finally retire, she held Aerten in her arms and let her cry for the life that she'd left behind, and then celebrate the life she now had.

"You've got me," Rina said, punctuating each word with a kiss. "You'll always have me."

"I love you," Aerten said. And kissed her wife back.

ACKNOWLEDGMENTS

This paperback has been a labour of love, and the two books within it might be the most emotional I've ever gotten whilst writing. So much in my life has changed since I started writing this series, and even more so since Value in Visions released. As ever, I could not have done it without the wonderful group of people who fill my life with so much joy and laughter, and who always remind me of my worth when I forget.

Special thanks go to Teresa, of Wolfsparrow Covers, for always making the most delicious covers; and to Randi, for formatting this for me.

To my Wordmakers: Coralie Moss, D Ann Williams, Rae Shawn, KK Hendin, Karmen Lee, Amanda Cinelli, Jordan Monroe, Lisa Kessler, Meka James, Elysabeth Grace, Fortune Whelan, and our leader, Tasha L. Harrison. You have been kind, and caring, and blunt with me when I ask you to be. I am a better writer because of you all, and a better person too.

To my Writing Coven: Stefanie Simpson, Aleksandr Voinov, Eden Bradley, Allysa Hart, Leslie Ayla, L. G. Knight, Holly March, Sarah E. Lily, Pippa Roscoe, Kiru Taye, Amy Andrews, and Talia Hibbert. I don't know what I have done to deserve such wonderfully talented friends, but I endeavour to always be worthy of your friendship.

To my anchor people: Sas, Harriet, Mary, Lotti, Jen, Beth, Oli and Thea; thank you for being such wonderful supports, and shouting encouragement at all times! Spending time with you and cooking for you all brings me so much joy.

To my new Brighton friends: Roisin, Bryony, Kit, Lucy, Benny, James, Ash, Robin, Lily, Sam, Raph, Amy and Bear; It is wild to me that I didn't know any of you a year ago, and now my life is so much richer for you all being a part of it. Thank you!

And there are so many friends who have called, visited, texted, and generally been good eggs throughout the last year: Ally, Chiara, Clare, Emily, Emily, Ewelina, Izzy, J Emery, Jenna, Jo H, Joanne, Katy, Kevin, Liam, Maria, Matt, Molly, Neha, Nick, Sarah BH, Sarah R, Tony, Veronica, Zaneta and so many more.

My family are as wild as the Baronis, and I love them all dearly. Rina's parents, aunt and uncle, and grandparents are all named after my own Italian grandparents and great-grandparents. The love that fills my life is in no small part due to you. You will always be remember and cherished. I love you.

And then there's Abi, my best friend and very own goofball. I am overwhelmed by your love and support, and I intend to always love you as you deserve – unreservedly, and with my whole heart.

And finally, dear reader, we come to you. I hope these stories bring you some joy, and remind to keep those you hold dear close.

LUNA AND MIA'S BOOK

The last thing Mia Baroni needed was a Goddess to upend her life. Luna keeps on trying to get her to go out at night and cavort by the light of the moon, and doesn't seem to grasp the concept of a 9 to 5 job. But there's something haunting in the Goddess's eyes, and Mia can't help but want to chase it away.

Welcome to the Godstouched Universe, where the Gods interfere in the lives of mortals. Blue Moon Magic is a sapphic romance between a human and a goddess, with a guaranteed Happy Ever After.

DIANA AND SILVANA'S BOOK

Silvana Baroni has been landed with a Goddess. Diana the Huntress, to be exact, which is more than a little awkward, considering that she's a vegetarian. That means all the standard courting rituals of the Huntress are out, but Silva realises that it'll take more than that to dissuade Diana from romancing her.

Welcome to the Godstouched Universe, where the Gods interfere in the lives of mortals. Blue Moon Magic is a sapphic romance between a human and a goddess, with a guaranteed Happy Ever After.

HECATE AND LILIANA'S BOOK

Hecate, Goddess of the Crossroads, is stalking Liliana Baroni. Well, maybe more attempting clumsily to romance her, than stalking. Still, Lili can't decide whether she should be frustrated or amused, especially when the Goddess's attentions bring with it interest from the Underworld.

Welcome to the Godstouched Universe, where the Gods interfere in the lives of mortals. Blue Moon Magic is a sapphic romance between a human and a goddess, with a guaranteed Happy Ever After.

START AT THE BEGINNING WITH THE FREED HUNT

Very little phases blacksmith Kenna, so accidentally awakening a Goddess barely gives her pause, until she discovers what gifts Belisama has bestowed in her. She finds herself in the midst of a power struggle between two Gods that she didn't even know existed, but it's the fact that this isn't a challenge she can face alone that will almost get her killed.

Morcant has been trapped as part of the Wild Hunt for centuries: he's seen his brother die as part of the curse; friends give up; and he'll do just about anything to keep the remaining members safe. So when he's promised their freedom, he agrees to do what the god Nodens asks, and stop the Godstouched from unwittingly creating more mayhem.

But the Godstouched is Kenna, the first woman to touch his heart in millennia, which leaves him with a horrendous choice: her happiness, or freedom for those he thinks of as family.

Welcome to the Godstouched Universe, where the Gods interfere in the lives of mortals. Forged in Flames is an m/f romance, with a guaranteed Happy Ever After.

ALSO FROM ALI WILLIAMS

The Softest Kinksters Collection collects short romances that capture snippets of kinky lives. From a subby himbo librarian, to married lesbians, to Dommes with ADHD, these kinksters use kink to alleviate anxiety, find connection, and to get off. Hard.

Includes a foreword by NYT Bestseller Eden Bradley, and a "Kink is Complicated" essay by Swoonies nominee Stefanie Simpson, as well as two new, exclusive stories!

ABOUT ALI

Ali Williams' inner romance reader is never quite satisfied, which is why she oscillates between writing romance, editing romance, and studying it as part of her PhD.

She can be found at the foot of the South Downs in the UK, either nerding out over local mythologies, reading tarot cards, or making homemade pasta, according to her Nanna's recipes.

She believes with all of her bifurious heart that writing romance is an act of rebellion and that academia will be so much better when studying diverse HEAs is naturally part of the curriculum.

Follow Ali on Twitter, Facebook, Instagram and TikTok, and sign up to her Newsletter!

Milton Keynes UK
Ingram Content Group UK Ltd.
UKHW040825111023
430376UK00004B/110